# W.i.t.c.h

Will    Irma    Taranee    Cornelia    Hay Lin

## A Weakened Heart

Adapted by ALICE ALFONSI

D0002290

© 2006 Disney Enterprises, Inc.

W.I.T.C.H. Will Irma Taranee Cornelia Hay Lin is a trademark of Disney Enterprises, Inc. Hyperion Paperbacks for Children is an imprint of Disney Children's Book Group, L.L.C.

Printed in the United States of America
First Edition
1 3 5 7 9 10 8 6 4 2

This book is set in 12/16.5 Hiroshige Book.
ISBN 0-7868-5595-9
Visit www.clubwitch.com

able to protect his own beloved Candracar.

Now that Nerissa had broken through its protected threshold, he could feel her darkness permeate the cloud-covered plane. With every step, she brought destruction closer, like storm winds approaching an open shoreline.

It is a desperate time, thought the Oracle, so it is time for desperate measures.

The Oracle turned toward Tibor. Standing before him, with his long, white beard and snow-white hair, his faithful servant appeared as worried as the Oracle himself.

I wish I could give Tibor better news, thought the Oracle. But there is nothing good in what I must convey.

"Nerissa is coming," he warned. "We have to defend ourselves. Quick! Summon the Elders. She must be forced to turn back."

With mixed feelings, the Oracle recalled the last time Nerissa had come to Candracar, so many years ago. Like Will, Nerissa had been selected as the Keeper of the Heart. But she had abused the trust that had been placed in her, using the Heart for her own selfish purposes.

Nerissa had betrayed her duty to the Oracle

and her fellow Guardians. So the Oracle had taken the Heart away from her. He gave it to a new Keeper, Nerissa's fellow Guardian Cassidy.

The Oracle's decision had enraged Nerissa. She could not stand to see Cassidy made the Keeper of her beloved Heart. So she had murdered the innocent Guardian.

The Oracle and the Elders of Candracar were outraged. They sentenced Nerissa to a living death. They sealed her in a tomb within Mount Thanos, a volcanic island surrounded by a glacial sea.

Everyone expected her sentence to last for eternity. But after centuries of imprisonment, Nerissa found herself released from her prison of fire and ice.

Unfortunately, Nerissa's punishment had not made her sorry for her crimes. Instead, she'd used the endless years inside Mount Thanos to plan her revenge. She'd honed her spells, drawing strength from the flow of the molten lava and the lapping water of the polar sea.

With her sorcery more powerful than ever, she'd located the new Keeper of the Heart. She'd waged war on Will and her fellow

Guardians. She'd entered their dreams to terrorize and weaken them. Finally, she'd tricked Will into giving her the Heart.

And now Nerissa is here in Candracar, thought the Oracle. His head was still throbbing from the booming impact of her arrival. He put his small hands to his temples and closed his eyes, willing the pain away.

If only I could will Nerissa away as easily, he thought.

By stealing the Heart, however, she had gained more power than he alone could defeat. And the Oracle knew exactly what would happen if Nerissa destroyed Candracar. Chaos would be unleashed on Earth and throughout the entire universe. Evil would be allowed to roam unchecked throughout the cosmos.

The Oracle had no desire to fight Nerissa. But he had no choice now. She was bringing her battle to the doorstep of his Temple. He had to rally the Council of Elders. Together they had to find a way to destroy Nerissa before she destroyed them.

"Call the mightiest Elders of the Congregation!" he again commanded Tibor. "Have them create the most impenetrable barrier that their powers can conceive!"

Tibor's deeply lined face creased even more with worry. The Oracle knew why: he had never before heard his master make such a request.

"What's happening, Oracle?" Tibor asked.

The Oracle answered with three simple words: "We're at war."

# TWO

"If somebody's dreaming," Will murmured on the back of her bicycle, "it sure isn't me—unfortunately!"

It seemed to Will that the last few days of her life *had* been a dream. On the other hand, she thought, *a total nightmare* would have been a more accurate description. At the moment, she was on her way to school. It was her first day back since Nerissa had tricked her into giving up the Heart.

Will had bundled herself well against the chilly air. A warm scarf was looped tightly around her neck, and she wore a thick sweater beneath her jacket. Still, Will couldn't help feeling a little shaky. She shivered as a gust of wind blew by her. It ruffled her mop of red hair and sent a pile of dry leaves swirling down the wide street.

This was one of her favorite parts of Heatherfield. It was quiet and pretty, with rows of century-old town houses lining the streets. Some had granite steps with wrought-iron railings. Others had big, old-fashioned windows. A few even had imposing stone gargoyles.

It actually cheered her up a bit to be biking to school that way. And, boy, did she need cheering up. She'd spent the last few days of her life hiding from everyone. She'd stayed home from school, pretending to have the flu. But hiding hadn't helped. She still felt terrible about failing so horribly.

She'd failed the Oracle, who had entrusted the Heart to her. She'd failed herself by being weak. And, worst of all, she'd failed her friends.

Because she no longer controlled the Heart, the powers of W.I.T.C.H.—Will, Irma, Taranee, Cornelia, and Hay Lin—were only a fraction of what they *should* have been. The Heart was what magnified each Guardian's separate elemental power. Irma's was water. Taranee's was fire. Cornelia's was earth. And Hay Lin's was air. But none of them could be Guardians anymore. Not without Will's control of the Heart's energy to unify and strengthen them.

Will sighed with self-disgust. Some Keeper I turned out to be, she thought.

The one thing that kept her going was the thought of the way her friends had reacted to her devastating failure. They had all chosen to *forgive* her. They had all chosen to stand behind her.

The fact that W.I.T.C.H. still had her back was the one thing that made her believe she might get the chance to make things right again. Slim to none, maybe, she figured, but there was still a *chance*!

I just can't give up now, she thought as she pumped her bike's pedals. I made a mistake, but I have to find the strength to learn from it and move on. The guys are counting on me, and if I give up now, I know I'll regret it for the rest of my life.

As Will rode along, she noticed that traffic was unusually light. That seemed odd to her. Heatherfield was a busy place, and traffic at that hour was usually bumper to bumper. But she didn't think much about it. She was too caught up gazing at the line of impressive town houses on either side of her.

Will wasn't from Heatherfield originally. She'd been born and raised further north, in a much smaller town. These old town houses reminded her of Fadden Hills. For sure, she thought, they had a lot more old-fashioned charm than the steel-and-glass skyscrapers of downtown Heatherfield.

"Whoa!" Will suddenly cried, clutching her hand brakes.

She'd just spied a very strange sight down a narrow alley. Thinking she might have imagined it, she backed her bike up to take a better look.

Where did this place come from? Will asked herself. Curious, she walked her bike along the passage and emerged into a large courtyard—*very* large. The whole space opened up to reveal a large, stately house.

"I never noticed such a pretty house here before," murmured Will.

The building in the courtyard looked just like one of those storybook houses back in Fadden Hills. It had dormer windows, a big brick chimney, and rustic shutters. It was the sort of home that belonged in the pages of a fairy-tale picture book. And it was covered in a beautiful blanket of *snow*!

Will was amazed. There'd been no snow on the streets or sidewalks of Heatherfield that morning. Yet here in this hidden courtyard, a beautiful mantle of white covered everything—the walkway, the trees, and the roof of the large, wood-framed home.

Will walked her bike up the path. With each step, her sneakers made that wintry crunching sound she'd always loved. Beautiful trees lined the pathway, their frosted leaves glistening in the morning light.

Once again, Will couldn't believe her eyes. The mature oaks and sycamores were impossibly big.

These are the sorts of trees you'd find in the deep woods, she thought, not the middle of Heatherfield! What is *up* with this place?

Will checked her watch. She didn't want to be late for school, but, on the other hand, she really wanted to find out who lived here. When she reached the front porch of the house, she leaned her bike against a post and peered into one of the mullioned front windows. Unfortunately, the glass was layered with grime, and she found it hard to see through.

*Hmmm,* she thought, I can't see anything from here.

*"Will?"*

The call was faint, but Will was certain she'd heard someone say her name. Or maybe it was some*thing.* Among her other Guardian powers, Will had discovered she had a bizarre talent for talking to machines. Maybe there was a TV set in there that wanted to talk, she thought, amused. Or a refrigerator with a really good story to tell.

Her heart began to race, but she told herself she wasn't scared . . . only curious. She walked up to the front door. She was about to knock when she saw that the door was slightly ajar.

*That's weird,* she thought. I'm sure it was shut tight when I first walked up the path.

"Hello? Can I come in?" Will called, slowly swinging the front door open wider. When it was open all the way, she peeked inside the house.

The room was empty. There was no furniture. The floor was completely bare, and exposed beams lined the ceiling. One end of the room held a smoke-stained fireplace. At the other was a flight of wooden stairs.

"Anybody home?" Will called. She listened for movement on the second floor. There wasn't a sound.

She was about to leave when she noticed a white fog creeping across the floor. It moved in a strange pattern, like the root system from one of those big old trees in the courtyard. Will followed the moving tendrils of fog to a rickety table she hadn't noticed before. It stood in a shadowy corner. On the table was a book.

"Oh," she murmured, "someone left a book behind. . . ."

Curious, she walked over to the table. She picked up the book to examine it. The volume was thick, heavy, and bound in leather. It looked very old. Will took a deep breath and blew dust off the cover . . . and then she *gasped*. The title read: *Il Triste Destino di Will*.

"Is—is this some kind of joke?" Will stammered.

She was no scholar. Not like Taranee. But Will had picked up enough foreign phrases at the Sheffield Institute to know what *Il Triste Destino di Will* meant: *Will's Unhappy Destiny*.

With a slightly shaky hand, she opened the

book. The pages were thick and edged in gold. It looked like one of those illuminated books from the Middle Ages she'd learned about in history class. The script was very ornate. And it was all in Latin. She looked closer at two illustrations—a female creature and a blond giant.

Something about the giant looked familiar. He wore blue armor over his bulging muscles. His yellow hair was shaggy. But it was his face that creeped Will out more than anything. It wasn't a normal human face. It was totally white and expressionless, as if the giant were wearing a mask—as if he were somebody's *puppet*.

Suddenly, the giant's eyes blinked. Then his mouth began to move. "Here you are, at last, Will!" he said, from inside the book. "We were getting bored, you know."

*Omigosh!* Will's eyes widened. She finally recognized the giant. It was Shagon, Nerissa's most powerful servant!

"So, have you decided to give up?" Shagon continued from within the book. "You have, haven't you? Wise choice!"

"How did you get here?" Will demanded, flinging the book away from her.

*Thump!*

"Hey!" Shagon complained as the book struck the floor. "Be gentle, now!"

Just then, the tendrils of white fog along the floor began to move again. They curled around the table's legs, climbing higher and higher, like slithering vines. Slowly, one tendril of fog changed color. At its base the tendril turned a deep burgundy. The top darkened into an inky black.

"You know, I'm tired of being thrown around by you!" declared a familiar voice from the transforming fog.

"Nerissa!" cried Will.

The sorceress had now fully materialized. Her eyes glowed blue. Her lips glistened blood red. And her long, black hair was draped around her like a vampire's cape.

Will rubbed her eyes. She pinched her arm. "This—this is another nightmare, isn't it?"

"For being the worst Guardian who ever set foot in Candracar, you're pretty sharp!" Nerissa said. Then she laughed, a screeching cackle that pierced Will's eardrums.

Shaking her head in horror, Will shrank back. The evil witch had terrorized her many times before, through her dreams. She'd terror-ized all the Guardians that way.

"I just came to thank you," Nerissa told Will. "Without your help, I would never be able to defeat you all!"

Behind Nerissa, two of her servants leaped from the pages of the book. The muscular giant Shagon shook his fist at Will. The demon woman Ember smiled evilly at her. Two more servants emerged from the creeping fog. There was a winged man made of ice and a snarling beast.

All four of Nerissa's servants appeared delighted with their mistress's victory. And, of course, so did the sorceress herself. "Look at yourself. You're through!" Nerissa taunted. "Are you ready to see me triumph?"

*No*, thought Will, *I'm not*!

That was when Will realized there was something really wrong with this picture. Hadn't Nerissa already won, by tricking Will into giving her the Heart? Why was she wasting time entering Will's dream like this? Just to gloat? That didn't make sense.

Will knew that Nerissa was obsessed with two things—the Heart and revenge. She'd already won the Heart back. But she had yet to exact her revenge on Candracar. . . . So why is she wasting time with me? Will wondered. *Unless* . . .

"Could Nerissa be worried?" Will whispered to herself. "Could the Guardians and I still pose a threat to her?"

Will's resolve strengthened with this realization. She felt a burst of confidence she hadn't known since she'd given away the Heart. She turned to Nerissa and pointed a threatening finger.

"You're a big talker, Nerissa. But the truth is that you're afraid you won't succeed, right?" Will challenged her. "Otherwise, why would you bother to come visit me again?"

The flash of doubt that passed over Nerissa's face was enough to make Will positively giddy! Clenching her fists and gritting her teeth, Will dug down deep. She searched inside herself. The Heart of Candracar was gone. She had lost it. The emptiness was almost too much to bear. But she hadn't lost *all* of her internal power. A well of energy was still there inside her!

She took a threatening step toward Nerissa. Using every ounce of power she could find within her being, she lashed out.

"You're history!" shouted Will. "Haven't you figured that out yet? You're not even strong enough to"—she felt a jolt—"trap me inside my dream!" She looked around. She was no longer inside the mysterious old house, shouting at Nerissa, but sitting up in bed, wearing her favorite striped pajamas.

With one punishing strike, Will had severed the sorceress's hold. Everything looked familiar to her now: her cozy bedroom furniture, her scuffed-up sneakers, the frog clock on her shelf—which currently read 3:10 A.M. Snapshots of her best friends were taped to the wall, along with a very special picture of her boyfriend, Matt Olsen.

The only thing missing was the Heart of Candracar. She'd escaped Nerissa, but she still had not been able to recover the Heart. Flopping back on her pillows, she felt totally defeated. Breaking away from Nerissa had felt good for a moment, but the reality was still a hard one to wake up to.

My dream may have ended, she thought with a miserable sigh, but as long as Nerissa has the Heart, my nightmare is far from over.

## THREE

Nerissa was absolutely furious! One moment she'd been in control of the little Guardian's dream, and the next—*pouf!*

"Ah! That blasted girl! She managed to escape!" Nerissa screeched.

She turned to face the servants by her side. Each was an extension of her dark magic. And she was still very proud of the way she'd created them.

Two had been fashioned from the elements around her own tomb. The winged female creature, Ember, had been formed out of the fiery ash of Mount Thanos's volcano. Tridart, the winged male, had been carved from the glacial ice on Thanos's polar shores.

Khor was Nerissa's third servant. The ferocious beast hadn't been fashioned from fire or ice. He had been transformed from a gentle dog that had been sniffing around the rim of Nerissa's volcanic prison. With a quick spell, she had ensnared him for her service.

When the dog's owner had come looking for him, Nerissa had acquired her fourth servant—Shagon. He had been a geologist, studying Nerissa's volcano. But she'd cast a powerful spell over him. Now, he was her mighty puppet.

As the only "human" under Nerissa's power, Shagon was her most powerful servant. But he was also the most difficult, especially when he tried to think for himself.

Still, Nerissa valued Shagon above the others. To him, she'd given a very special ability—the power to feed on hate. This was what fueled Shagon. The more his opponents raged at him, the stronger he became.

In Nerissa's view, her four dark servants were an undefeatable army. With them by her side and with the Heart of Candracar under her control, Nerissa knew she could not fail. And yet, Will had been able to escape her enchanted nightmare. Nerissa couldn't explain that. Even worse, the little brat's final words had pricked Nerissa like sharp thorns in her side: *Haven't you figured that out yet? You're not even strong enough . . .*

Not strong enough! Nerissa repeated it to herself in outrage. Not strong enough! Nerissa would never admit the truth to her four faithful servants. But a part of her was secretly worried that Will was right.

I'm so close to my goal, she thought. So close to making the Oracle and the Elders pay for burying me alive in that blasted mountain! The *last* thing I need is interference from those tiresome little Guardians!

Nerissa knew that the Guardians had not been defeated.

That was why she had to keep checking on them. Despite losing the Heart, Will still possessed a vital power inside her. All of the Guardians did.

"That's it," Nerissa told her servants. "I went too easy on Will and her friends!" She turned to face the snarling beast she'd transformed from a mere dog. "If they try to stop me again, show no mercy, Khor!"

"*Grrrrrrr. . . .*" the beast growled in reply,

indicating his compliance with the order.

"And now," Nerissa continued with an evil grin, "back to our regularly scheduled program of revenge!"

Clapping her hands, Nerissa ended the spell of the nightmare. Instantly, she and her servants were no longer in Will's mysterious Heatherfield dream house. They were back among the clouds of Candracar's ethereal plane.

With renewed determination, the small band continued their march toward the Temple of Candracar. Before long, the clouds around them grew thicker. Walking became more difficult, like wading through waist-deep cotton. Nerissa scanned the horizon and discovered the reason.

Not far away, a monstrous spire rose up from Candracar's clouds. Like a crystal cactus, each level of the tall spire displayed an array of curving spikes. Just the sight of those ugly spikes made her blood boil.

"I remember this place: the Tower of Mists," she told her servants. "Those hypocrites of the Congregation! They don't even have the courage to call it by its real name."

"What is its real name?" asked Shagon, gazing at the bony crystal spikes.

"That's the *prison* of Candracar," Nerissa informed him. She assumed the mists and clouds were thick there for one reason. The Elders didn't want to see it from their precious Temple. *Typical of their hypocrisy,* she thought. They didn't wish to be reminded that ugliness could exist in their beautiful dimension.

"A prison with chains and locks," Shagon said. "Not even this dimension of peace is immune to the power of hate!"

Facing Shagon, Nerissa looked deep into his enchanted eyes. She could still see his human consciousness.

"Don't talk about peace, Shagon," she said. There is no serenity in Candracar. You have no idea how many secrets are hidden inside the walls of the Temple."

Nerissa furiously clenched her fists. They all think they are so high-and-mighty, she thought, but they are just as guilty as I am for everything that's happened!

"In pursuit of what they call a 'higher good,' the Congregation is willing to engage in acts of evil," Nerissa spat. "In the name of what he calls *justice*, the Oracle has committed terrible wrongs."

The great "seer" should have foreseen what the Heart would do to me, Nerissa thought. He should have foreseen what would happen when he gave the Heart to Cassidy. . . . Yes, I killed my fellow Guardian. But how dare the Oracle have the gall to punish me so cruelly when he failed to punish *himself*!

That gall, that hypocrisy, was what Nerissa planned to make the Oracle finally face. The Congregation and all of Candracar would face it, too.

I will have my revenge, she thought. For their centuries of hypocrisy, I will wage war upon them all!

"The Oracle's errors are locked away within that tower," she told Shagon as she pointed to the prickly prison. "When the Temple is mine, I might just reveal its true nature."

Deep down, however, Nerissa wondered whether she'd really be able to look into that abyss. . . .

As her thoughts trailed off, Nerissa saw a slight movement within the Temple. Even at this distance, she knew any Elders inside would have been able to see her.

They're probably sounding the alarms, she thought with a smirk. But they'll soon find it's too late. I have already entered their dimension. The hour of battle is here.

# FOUR

Sitting in first-period math, Cornelia cringed. The class was already well under way when Will stumbled into the room. It was hardly a grand entrance. To Cornelia, it looked more like a horror show.

First of all, the former Keeper of the Heart appeared to have gotten dressed in the dark. Her cotton shirt was buttoned wrong, her sweater was inside out, and the wings of her collar were totally wrinkled. The words *fashion disaster* definitely came to mind.

Second—the hair. Will usually had that shag rocker thing going on. Not that there was anything *wrong* with that. After all, her boyfriend was the lead singer in a totally hot band called Cobalt Blue. But this morning, Will looked as if she were fronting a band called Bad Hair Day.

*Sheesh,* Cornelia thought. I know this whole losing-the-Heart thing's been really hard on the girl, but the least she could do is run a comb across her head!

The third thing that made Cornelia cringe was the whole tardy act. Will was never a big rise-and-shiner. But the girl had missed home-room *and* the first twenty minutes of her first class. Maybe that was okay back in "Nowhere Hills," but it was no way to get on the honor roll at Heatherfield's Sheffield Institute.

"Um . . . s—sorry, Mr. Horseberg," Will stammered with a sheepish grin.

The math teacher adjusted his rectangular glasses. He looked down the long nose of his long, horsey face. "Your company is always an honor, Miss Vandom," he said drily.

Will's face flushed red. She gritted her teeth in a forced grin and slunk over to her desk. Cornelia cringed again. She wondered if this moment could have been any *more* embarrassing.

"Hi," Will whispered. Her desk was right in front of Cornelia's.

Oh, my gosh, Cornelia thought. She immediately took back every snarky thing she'd just thought about her friend. Finally seeing Will up close, Cornelia realized that the problems with her friend's appearance went far beyond her fashion *backward* wardrobe.

Her cheeks were sunken, her skin appeared sallow, and she had bags under her eyes. Cornelia knew Will had only been faking the flu at home. But right now she looked totally exhausted, as if she'd *really* been fighting an illness—

Or maybe, Cornelia realized, Will had been fighting something else. . . .

"Another nightmare?" Cornelia asked.

Will nodded as she slipped into her seat. "Nerissa again."

Cornelia waited for their teacher to turn his back and begin writing on the chalkboard. Then she leaned forward and tapped Will on the shoulder. She had some news that might actually perk the poor girl up.

"Eric wants to see us at the observatory," Cornelia whispered. "It's about Halinor's diary. Sounds like there's news."

Will nodded, her expression brightening.

Cornelia knew she should have left it at that. But she just couldn't keep herself from adding, "And straighten your collar!"

After school that day, Cornelia met up with the rest of the Guardians. Together they took a bus to Heatherfield Park, where Heatherfield Observatory was located.

It was almost impossible to miss the observatory. Its domed roof rose high above the trees on a rise called Heather Hill. The building itself looked like a grand monument. The walls were white granite, and the windows were tall and stately. But Cornelia's favorite feature was the line of classic columns. Like ivory soldiers, they surrounded the building, as if they were standing guard at its perimeter.

"This place reminds me a little of the Temple in Candracar," Cornelia told the other Guardians.

"Except for the fact that it's *not* in a weird dimension surrounded by a bunch of clouds," Irma joked, craning her neck to see the top of the dome. "And I doubt very much we'll find an all-seeing Oracle in this joint!"

The girls climbed the white stone steps and

pushed through the large front doors. Hay Lin spoke to a security guard at a desk in the lobby. He smiled and beckoned them over to the main staircase.

The wide marble steps went up several floors. The girls climbed and climbed until they reached a spiral staircase; they kept following Hay Lin up and up and up. Just when Cornelia thought her legs were going to fall off, they reached the top. Hay Lin waved them all through a single door.

"If I see one more step," threatened Irma, gulping deep breaths of air, "I'm going to scream."

"You won't have to," said Hay Lin. "We're here."

*Here* turned out to be the office of the astronomer Zachary Lyndon. In one corner of the room stood a desk with a computer and a table with star maps spread across it. At the other end of the room, the ceiling opened up into a giant dome. Below the dome sat a huge telescope.

"Hi, Eric!" called Hay Lin, waving excitedly.

Cornelia smiled. Of course Hay Lin would be excited to see Eric, she thought. He was her crush. Tall and lanky, he had kind eyes and a really friendly smile. Cornelia figured he was pretty cute—just not as cute as her own true love, Caleb.

Cornelia, Will, Taranee, and Irma followed Hay Lin over to the telescope, where they all greeted Eric Lyndon and his grandfather.

Cornelia had never been to the observatory before. But she figured Eric's grandfather looked pretty much the way an astronomy professor should look. He wore a white lab coat and thick, horn-rimmed glasses. His longish gray hair was brushed back from his wrinkled forehead. And his bushy eyebrows had nothing on his woolly mustache. It drooped over his mouth like the whiskers of a wise walrus.

Professor Lyndon sat in a red swivel chair in front of the telescope. It was *the* biggest tele scope Cornelia had ever seen, with huge gears and mechanisms attached to every corner.

The viewfinder was easy enough to figure out. *Duh,* Cornelia thought. You look through the viewfinder and you see the stars, right?

What wasn't so easy to figure out was the high-tech equipment around the telescope. There were at least two computer screens, a keypad, and countless buttons, dials, and gauges.

Irma stepped up and pointed. "Wow! That's some toy! What do all those gizmos do?"

Cornelia rolled her eyes. Leave it to Irma to miss the point entirely. They weren't there for an astronomy lesson. What they needed right now was some words of wisdom. That was what they hoped to get from the diary of Halinor, who had once been a Guardian, just like them.

It turned out that Halinor had been watching over Will for years. Will had been pretty freaked out about that when she found out. It had been a well-kept secret. But when Halinor passed away, she had left the diary for Will to read.

Unfortunately, Will couldn't read it. The pages were filled with strange symbols. There were stars, planets, and constellations. None of the Guardians had been able to figure it out.

That was why Hay Lin had taken it to Eric. He was probably the smartest kid they knew. And he'd been studying astronomy there at the observatory. When he couldn't figure out how to translate it, he took it to his grandfather.

At the moment, the professor was smiling

patiently at Irma. She was still waiting for an answer to her "gizmos" question.

"Young lady," he said, "if you're that interested in astronomy, you should sign up for our summer course next year."

Irma tapped her chin in thought. "Is math involved?"

"Most definitely," said the professor.

"Um . . . maybe I'm not so interested," Irma mumbled, stepping back.

Cornelia suppressed a laugh. It looked as though the water Guardian's enthusiasm had just been doused!

"What about the diary, Professor?" Hay Lin politely asked.

Eric's grandfather nodded his head and picked up the leather-bound book. "I hadn't translated Runic since my university days. But I managed to solve your riddle."

All the girls exchanged excited glances. Finally, thought Cornelia. We're *finally* going to learn something useful!

Will stepped forward. "Please don't keep us on pins and needles, Professor Lyndon."

The old man nodded. "If you were hoping to discover incredible secrets, I'll have to disappoint you. Although I was able to decipher the journal, I'm afraid it only amounts to a collection of senseless notes and symbols."

The girls exchanged glances again—disappointed ones this time.

"What do you mean by 'senseless'?" Will asked.

The professor pushed up his horn-rimmed glasses. "The diary contains a long series of astronomical calculations dating back to over a century and a half ago—"

"—And the coordinates of an unknown constellation!" said Eric, jumping in excitedly.

Cornelia noticed that Eric looked directly at Hay Lin as he spoke. He was obviously trying to impress her.

It seemed that Professor Lyndon had come to the same conclusion. He raised a bushy eyebrow at his grandson, then shifted his own gaze to Hay Lin. "*Hmmm,*" he said with suppressed amusement, "I might have used more technical terms to tell you the same thing, but my impatient grandson has preempted me."

"Are you sure?" Will asked.

The professor nodded and waved them over. They watched as he swiveled to face the huge telescope's display panel. He flipped a switch and turned a knob.

*Bzzzzzzzzz!*

The girls looked up to see the great dome above them sliding open. The lens of the telescope was now pointed directly at the orange late-afternoon sky.

"I calculated every possible shift and variation," the professor said as he tapped commands on the keypad. "But in that particular portion of the sky, I found nothing relevant."

He swiveled around to face them again. "Later on, I'll make another attempt. But to be honest, I'm not very hopeful."

Will's shoulders slumped.

She looks so defeated, Cornelia thought. This is terrible!

Stepping closer, Cornelia put a reassuring hand on Will's shoulder and gently squeezed. Will gave her a grateful glance.

"Can I take a look, Professor?" Irma asked. She rushed up to the viewfinder and bent over to look through it.

Cornelia rolled her eyes. Somebody say, "math" again, she thought. That should get Irma to back off!

The professor appeared amused by Irma's rekindled enthusiasm. He shook his head and said, "Perhaps you've never noticed . . . but it seems that stars are more easily seen at *night*, if that's what you're trying to do."

"*Um* . . . oh, I knew that, of course!" Irma quickly assured him. She paused a moment, then added, "In any case, are you sure you didn't make a mistake?"

The professor folded his arms. "Unlike *you*, young lady, I never make mistakes!"

Cornelia shook her head, and Taranee cringed. The look in their eyes said it all: water girl has reached a whole new level of rudeness!

As Will stepped up to thank the professor, Irma walked over to Cornelia and jerked her thumb in his direction. "What's with him?" she asked. "Was he offended or something?"

Cornelia held up her hand. "Do us a favor, Irma," she whispered. "Keep *quiet*."

Over at the telescope, the professor passed Will the leather-bound journal. "Here's your diary back," he said. "If it was all a joke, it was certainly a very elaborate one."

"It's no joke, sir," Will assured him.

The professor sighed. "Well, I combed

through every inch of the sky . . . but there was no trace of that star Cassidy."

Will's eyes widened. "C—Cassidy."

"Yes, I'd forgotten. *Cassidy*," Professor Lyndon explained. "That's the name of the non-existent star the diary describes."

Will looked absolutely stricken. And Cornelia knew why. The room fell silent for a few moments; then the professor said he had nothing more to tell them, and the Guardians moved toward the exit.

"Thanks for everything, Professor Lyndon," Will called.

Cornelia and the other girls thanked him, too. They all headed for the top of the spiral staircase—all except Hay Lin. Cornelia turned back to find her still talking with Eric.

"I'm sorry, Hay Lin," he quietly told her. "I was hoping I could help you."

Hay Lin smiled and touched his arm. "And that's just what you did, Eric. Thanks again."

The Guardians exited the observatory the way they had come. They climbed down the spiral staircase, descended the marble steps, and pushed through the heavy front doors.

After descending the steps out front, they

found themselves back among the trees and paths of Heatherfield Park. But they didn't walk far. Will sat down heavily on the first bench she saw. Taranee plopped down beside her, dropping her head between her hands. Irma draped herself over the back of the bench, and Cornelia stood beside Will in the chilly air.

"Well?" said Cornelia, shoving her hands into the pockets of her sky blue coat. "Isn't anybody going to say something?"

"What is there to say?" said Will. "You heard it for yourself. . . . *Cassidy*."

Cornelia sighed. She knew who Cassidy was, of course. All of them did. Cassidy had served as a fellow Guardian with Halinor. Cassidy was also the Keeper of the Heart who'd been murdered by Nerissa.

But a nonexistent star named Cassidy didn't mean much to Cornelia. And she could tell by the confused looks on everybody's faces that it didn't mean much to them, either.

"Cassidy," Will whispered. "Cassidy."

Suddenly, Will's expression began to change. And Cornelia could tell that in her mind she was turning something over and over again.

Will is figuring out our next move, Cornelia realized. That's a good thing, since I don't have a clue what to do next. I just hope whatever she's got in mind doesn't involve breaking and entering!

"Hey, guys," said Hay Lin, catching up to them.

Cornelia would have asked where Hay Lin had been, but she already knew. She'd lagged behind on the front steps of the observatory to talk to Eric a little longer.

The chemistry between Eric and Hay Lin was impossible to miss. Cornelia was in love herself, so it was easy for her to recognize the signs. All through their meeting with the professor, Hay Lin and Eric had been stealing glances at each other.

The air Guardian was actually the last member of W.I.T.C.H. to have developed a crush on a boy. Until then, Hay Lin had thought boys were a silly waste of time.

Well, thought Cornelia, after seeing the girl totally smitten with Eric today, I'd say she doesn't feel that way anymore!

Cornelia was really glad that Hay Lin had a boyfriend. But seeing Hay Lin and Eric exchanging special looks and little touches made Cornelia's heart ache. She missed her own boyfriend desperately. With every fiber of her being she wished *she* could be exchanging little looks and touches with Caleb just then.

But Caleb was not the sort of boyfriend who could hang with Cornelia in the halls of Sheffield. He couldn't call her on the phone, or take her to the movies. In fact, at that moment, Caleb wasn't even there on the earth!

He was a being from another dimension, a brave rebel who'd risked his life to save his world of Metamoor. And, for the past few months, Caleb had been floating in a healing room located in the Temple of Candracar. He was recovering from an assault by Nerissa.

The evil sorceress had kidnapped Caleb and nearly killed him. He'd survived her attack but been completely stripped of his memory.

The Guardians had found Caleb and taken him to Candracar. The Oracle had placed him in the Cosmos of Abeyance. There, in a vortex of cosmic energies, he was still struggling to reconnect with the memories of his life.

Cornelia knew this wasn't exactly your typical boyfriend-girlfriend relationship. But she loved Caleb, so she was willing to be patient.

More than anything, she wanted to be with him again. For now, however, she had to accept that the best thing for the boy she loved was to float in a room full of nothingness, in a dimension far away.

# FIVE

*Cornelia . . .*

The word fluttered lazily through Caleb's mind like the plume of a delicate bird.

*Cornelia . . .*

Again and again the word sounded . . . until Caleb realized that the word was a name, one that evoked a particular image. . . .

A young woman suddenly appeared before him. She stood tall and confident. Her skin was luminous. Her long hair flowed down her slender body like a golden waterfall. Her purple-and-turquoise wings appeared as fragile as flower petals. But with them, Caleb knew she could fly with the strength of ten eagles.

*Cornelia . . .*

She was a Guardian.

Her eyes were bluer than the lakes of his home world, and her heart was braver than a lion's.

He longed to reach out with his fingers to touch her skin, stroke her cheek. But he felt nothing, only air. The young woman he loved had vanished.

For months now, Caleb had been able to see Cornelia only this way—as a memory, a dream image. He'd been floating on a bed of cosmic currents, his muscular arms and legs buoyed by the energy around him.

This room, this Cosmos of Abeyance, was a place of nothingness. Months ago, that nothingness had been within Caleb, too. Gradually, however, the pieces of his past had floated back to him in shreds and snippets, in and out of order. . . .

He saw visions of Metamoor's rolling hills and fog-shrouded valleys. He saw its rustic farms. He saw the Gothic buildings and stone fountains of Meridian, its capital city.

Caleb remembered that his beautiful world was now at peace. But he also remembered that it hadn't always been that way. A frightening image suddenly came to him: the image of a man with long, flaxen hair and a small red goatee. He wore fine robes and a glittering crown, but his features were twisted with greed and anger.

*Phobos . . .*

Caleb flinched as he recognized the evil prince. Even in the sleep of the Cosmos of Abeyance, his body stiffened with tension, his pulse raced with adrenaline.

"Phobos," Caleb whispered with disgust.

Caleb had always despised Phobos and all that the sorcerer stood for. In his lust for power, Phobos had used fear and intimidation to terrorize his own people. He'd even tried to make Caleb a part of that terror.

The weak, the sick, the old, the young—it never mattered who you were in Metamoor. If you spoke against Phobos, his army would come to your house, burn it down, and throw you into the prince's dungeons.

To find the so-called traitors, Phobos used colorful spies called Murmurers. The Murmurers were wraiths that had been transformed by magic from the flowers in the prince's palace garden.

*That is what I was . . .*

With stunning clarity, Caleb suddenly

remembered his first form . . . petals and a stem, roots in the ground. He remembered the feel of the dew on his petals, the warmth of his home world's sunlight.

He'd begun his life as a flower. And one day, the dark prince had used powerful magic to transform him. He remembered growing and growing, higher and higher, his stem splitting and becoming legs. He remembered his arms taking shape, as well as his neck and his head. He remembered blinking and for the first time opening his big brown eyes.

But Caleb also remembered resisting the will of his dark master. Phobos had expected him to slink through the city streets, combing the countryside. He had wanted Caleb to spy on the people of Metamoor. But after Caleb had witnessed the ugly violence against his fellow Metamoorians, he'd refused to serve the prince in any way.

Instead, Caleb had joined the rebels who were fighting to free Metamoor from the prince's dark tyranny. Caleb's form had begun to change again, but this time not through magic. His own will and determination had transformed him into a human.

The rebellion had been a hard, long fight. And in his sleep in the Cosmos of Abeyance, Caleb began to remember that he had not fought alone. There'd been many brave souls who'd fought beside him. Many familiar faces came back to him, including . . .

"Vathek," Caleb whispered. His heart leaped at the memory of his big, blue friend.

More faces came to him. And none had fought more bravely and truly than the Guardians from the world of the earth. *What had they called themselves? Oh, yes!*

"W.I.T.C.H." he whispered.

There was Will with her bright, determined eyes and sleek red hair. Will was the leader, the Keeper of the Heart of Candracar. There was Irma, the impish water Guardian, who liked to joke and tease. There was Taranee, the fire Guardian, the serious girl, who wore large round glasses and braids in her dark brown hair. There was Hay Lin, the air Guardian, whose blue-black pigtails sailed behind her as she soared on the wind. And, finally, there was . . .

"Cornelia."

With one whisper of her sweet name,

Cornelia's image returned to Caleb. Memories of their time together began to flow over him like the invigorating waters of a mountain stream. . . .

*Be safe.*

Those two words came to Caleb's mind . . . but why?

*Be safe.*

"Of course!" Caleb whispered. He remembered now! That's what he'd told Cornelia, just before their final battle against Phobos. He had looked deep into her sapphire blue eyes and felt the power of her love. The heavy sword in his hand had grown instantly lighter in that moment. The courage in his heart had been strengthened beyond words.

*"Be safe,"* he'd said, and then they'd both gone into battle.

Bravely and fiercely they'd fought against Phobos and his army. Caleb remembered that fiery collision between good and evil. Even now, the corded muscles in Caleb's arms twitched as he relived the clash.

"So I guess it's true," Phobos had said, deflecting blow after blow from Caleb's broadsword. "You're a traitor. You've gone and turned against your master. . . ."

"You're not master of anything, Phobos," Caleb had told him, "and definitely not the master of me. Nothing you see around you is yours!"

"And to think that you were once a poor Murmurer . . ." Phobos had said.

"Wrong!" Caleb had cried. "I was a Murmurer capable of reason. When I finally opened my eyes, I knew right away what side I should be on."

"A Murmurer with a will of its own is a mistake," Phobos had said, "and there's only one thing to do with mistakes. . . ."

"*No-o-o-o-o-o-o!*"

Phobos had struck out with a devastating bolt of energy. The dark magic had enveloped Caleb.

"Caleb!"

Cornelia had cried out, but it was too late. The prince's magic had transformed Caleb back into his flower form again. He'd gone back to being nothing but a delicate lily with white petals and a green stem.

The rebels had won their battle that day. Elyon, the new queen of Metamoor, had taken her place as its new and rightful ruler. But Caleb had lost his precious human form. He had lost his chance at love, at life, at happiness.

Caleb recalled how Cornelia had gently gathered him into her hands and taken him back to her world. She'd placed his stem in water, kept his white petals safe in her bedroom. She'd cared for him, talked to him, cried over him. And Caleb had heard every word. He had not been able to see her, but he'd felt every gentle touch of her fingers, every anguished tear.

Finally, Cornelia had found a way to bring him back to his human form again. By a twist of fate, she had come to possess all five Guardian powers. Instead of giving them back to Candracar, however, she'd given Caleb everything she'd come to possess. It had been a crime against Candracar, a complete violation of the Oracle's rules, but Cornelia hadn't cared.

Her sacrifice had worked. Once Caleb was given the five Guardian powers, he'd grown back his human legs, arms, and body. But, sadly, he had not *become* human again. He had merely transformed back into a Murmurer, a simple wraith from Phobos's evil garden.

Caleb knew that, in such a state, the Oracle and the Council of Elders would have placed him in Candracar's prison. And they would have been right to do so. As a Murmurer he'd been a vessel for evil, a mere extension of the prince's dark magic.

It was Cornelia's teardrop that had brought Caleb back to what he'd once been. The single drop against his Murmurer's green flesh had transformed him into a human again. And Caleb remembered why. . . .

"If we have loved each other in our dreams," he had told her, back on the day they'd first met, "the Veil between our worlds will not be able to divide us. . . ."

When he'd said those words to her, Cornelia had begun to cry. And Caleb had caught her teardrop on his finger.

"Do you know what this is?" he'd said to her. "It is a promise. A promise that one day we'll meet again. . . ."

It was the presence of that promise in his heart, the memory of that first teardrop from Cornelia's eyes, that had transformed Caleb the second time.

"Your teardrop . . . within me . . . forever . . ."

Now, in his healing sleep, Caleb remembered that he owed Cornelia more than his love. He owed her his life. The memory of her sacrifice was now pulsing through his being, just as another memory came back to him—the memory of his own sacrifice for her.

The Council of Elders had called Cornelia up to Candracar to be judged and punished for misusing the Guardian powers. Caleb remembered how fragile she'd looked that day, standing before the Council, so vulnerable, so fearful of what the Elders would rule.

That was when Caleb had stepped up to address the Council himself. He remembered the faces of all the strange beings from so many worlds. Everyone had been shocked that Caleb had dared to interrupt the proceedings. But Caleb had refused to back down. He had boldly offered himself in exchange for any punishment set forth for Cornelia. . . .

"I will remain in the Temple as your servant," he'd promised them.

The Council had accepted Caleb's offer. They had made him the Herald of Candracar. And Caleb had been forced to part with

Cornelia once more. She'd returned to her life in Heatherfield. And he'd stayed behind in Candracar to serve the Oracle and the Congregation.

But Caleb and Cornelia had parted from each other this time with happiness in their hearts. Both had been confident that they would see each other again before long. Then Nerissa had robbed Caleb of every memory of Cornelia's sweet face.

*Until now . . .*

Faster and faster, Caleb felt his memories flooding back. Not just the big ones but the small ones, too. He clenched his fists as he recalled every battle he'd fought on Metamoor, every punch he'd thrown, every thrust of his sword.

The Cosmos of Abeyance seemed to be regenerating him in record time, lighting up his vital spark with great urgency. With his eyes still closed, Caleb felt the last fragments of memory returning.

Now, after all that time floating in Candracar, Caleb could finally recall Nerissa's vicious attack and the reason for it. The evil sorceress had wanted the five Guardian powers that Cornelia had placed inside of him. And when she'd taken those powers from Caleb, she'd cruelly and brutally stripped him of his identity, too.

"Nerissa," Caleb rasped.

Although he was still sleeping, Caleb suddenly knew. . . .

*Nerissa is near.*

He sensed her presence right there in Candracar. That must have been why his healing was accelerating, he thought. He was needed.

With a war about to start, Candracar's cosmic energies were clearly urging Caleb to remember what he'd once been, what he would always be . . . a warrior.

# SIX

As-Sharwa was one of the oldest residents of the mystical dimension of Candracar, and one of the wisest. His elongated forehead was tattooed with mystical runes. His long gray hair fell to the sides and far below his narrow, wrinkled face. Yet despite his advanced age, he stood strong and tall.

Hundreds of Elders watched in silence from the gallery of the Great Hall as As-Sharwa approached the Oracle. The vast chamber was so quiet that the only sound was the rustle of the old man's silken robes.

The Oracle did not appear to sense As-Sharwa's approach. Lost in a cosmic trance, he floated above the golden platform at the center of the mist-shrouded floor. His legs were folded under him in a lotus position. His arms were spread wide, his palms turned up.

As-Sharwa waited patiently for the wisest of the wise to acknowledge his presence. He felt confident in his role as the elected Voice of the Congregation. All of the Elders of Candracar were present in the renowned hall. But only As-Sharwa was permitted to address the Oracle at that moment.

As he waited to speak, As-Sharwa could feel the tension mounting inside him. Although his eyes were bright and intense, they were also filled with worry. He had no doubts that his face was projecting apprehension, his brow becoming furrowed with anxiety.

He knew that Nerissa was coming. She would soon be there, at the center of the Temple of Candracar. But as dire as the situation had become, Nerissa's coming was not As-Sharwa's only fear—the Oracle's plans for defending Candracar frightened As-Sharwa as much as the renegade Guardian herself. Perhaps more.

Now, As-Sharwa waited to voice his misgivings to the Oracle, who was still floating placidly above his golden platform. As-Sharwa tried once again to think, to plan, to find a way out of the deadly dilemma they all faced.

But after much contemplation, As-Sharwa could see no way out. Only the Oracle can save us, he thought, if he does not destroy us in the process.

"I am listening, As-Sharwa," the Oracle suddenly said.

As-Sharwa was caught by surprise. He looked up to find the Oracle calmly regarding him.

"You may speak," the Oracle said. "What is the opinion of the Congregation?"

As-Sharwa sighed deeply; his eyes had a haunted look. "We are ready, Oracle. But I must ask if you are truly prepared to let loose the destructive power of the Resonance against Nerissa."

For a long moment, the Oracle silently considered As-Sharwa's question. Then he focused his gaze intently on the old man's face. It took all of As-Sharwa's mental abilities, all of his will, not to shrink back in awe and fear under the Oracle's stare.

"What is your concern?" the Oracle demanded. His voice was a quiet explosion of power that filled the chamber.

"That the remedy will be worse than the illness," As-Sharwa bravely replied.

The Oracle patiently nodded, allowing As-Sharwa to continue. "It could be a complete catastrophe," the Voice of the Congregation warned. "The frequency of the Resonance could devastate the Temple of Candracar itself. And if that happened, Nerissa would be the least of our worries."

There was a collective gasp from the Elders. And, for a moment, the Oracle remained silent. Then the clouds underneath him dispersed. The Oracle drifted down to the golden platform at the center of the floor of the chamber. As soon as his bare feet touched the cold surface, the Oracle turned from As-Sharwa to address the assembly.

"Listen to me, Brethren of the Congregation," the Oracle began. "I am aware of the risk I have asked you to face. But I ask you once again to trust me!"

Once more, the Elders muttered among themselves.

"Nerissa is steps away from Candracar," the Oracle continued. "She must be stopped before calamity engulfs us all. The effect of the Resonance is our only hope!"

Silently, the assembled Elders contemplated the Oracle's words. One by one, they nodded in agreement. Only As-Sharwa hesitated, but just for a moment. Once the seer turned around and set his burning gaze on the old man, As-Sharwa nodded, too.

The Oracle lifted his arms to the heavens, setting his jaw with new determination. "We must not waver," he told the assembly. "Therefore, concentrate, and do not fear. Do everything in your power to control the forces we unleash. Direct them against Nerissa and her evil minions."

The Oracle waved to the beings around him. The Elders came down from their seats. They gathered close to the Oracle and As-Sharwa, forming a huge circle. As one, they closed their eyes and bowed their heads.

As-Sharwa bowed his head, too. Then, slowly, he channeled the Resonance, raising his arm and lifting his palm upward.

For a long moment, nothing happened. Then a dull hum began, barely discernible at first to human ears. The sound gradually increased in volume so that it resembled the subtle sound of a hummingbird's wings. The buzz continued to intensify. It grew louder and louder until the reverberations made the Elders' teeth chatter and their heads throb.

Through their combined willpower, the Elders shut out the sound that battered their ears, and they blocked the pain that threatened to overwhelm them. They concentrated intensely, working together to contain and focus the incredible powers that had just been unleashed.

The Resonance was just a deafening roar now, a mighty noise that shook the crystal assembly chamber and everything beyond. Still the sound increased in volume. The Temple's crystal columns cracked, and its windows shattered.

Fighting to control the powerful shock wave, As-Sharwa's brain seemed to expand even as his body grew weaker from the battering. In his mind's eye he could almost see Nerissa and her evil servants standing within sight of Candracar's gate. He imagined the overwhelming force of the Resonance washing over them. He knew Nerissa could do nothing now but cover her ears and scream.

Surely, she will fall, he thought. The man of ice who serves her will crumble into shards. The wings on her fiery female demon will shrivel and fall away.

Meanwhile, the walls of the Temple continued to quiver around the Elders. But though they shook with the full power of the Resonance, they did not fall.

As-Sharwa soon felt the dark resistance fading beyond the Temple walls. He sensed Nerissa's evil presence lessening. It grew smaller and smaller until it disappeared completely.

*We've won!* thought As-Sharwa in joy.

He halted the Resonance. The Elders fell to their knees. Exhausted sighs filled the chamber. Tibor caught As-Sharwa before he collapsed.

"Take heart, Voice of the Congregation," Tibor cried. "It held! The Temple is still standing. We did it!"

Despite his physical weakness, As-Sharwa's eyes were bright, and his voice was strong. "It was exhausting! Nerissa and her companions fought to the very end, but we won."

The Elders all looked to the Oracle for

confirmation. But he only frowned. "No, unfortunately, Nerissa is still alive," the Oracle said. "She and her creatures fell, it is true. But now they are rising again."

The chamber erupted with fearful cries. But the commotion died down when the Elders saw a new being stride confidently into the chamber, someone they had never expected to see so soon—the Herald of Candracar!

Young Caleb was clad in a belted white tunic. His dark hair was long and shaggy, as if it hadn't been cut in some time. His skin color appeared very pale, as though he had not seen any sun for months. But beneath his long bangs, his brown eyes burned with a supernatural fire.

"Caleb!" Tibor cried. "Who woke you from your sleep in the Cosmos of the Abeyance? What are you doing here?"

"I want to join you," Caleb declared.

Tibor shook his head and opened his mouth to protest, but the Oracle stepped between them.

"Your offer is a generous one," the Oracle told Caleb. "But you aren't ready yet. You are too weak to take on Nerissa and her creatures."

"No! You're wrong," said Caleb, standing his ground. His legs still felt a little shaky, but he was determined to do his part in the upcoming battle. "I'm better now, Oracle. And I'll prove it to you if you give me the chance."

# SEVEN

Irma shook her head in astonishment. Will was the only person she knew who could strike up a close personal relationship with an electronic device.

*Click!*

The big, heavy double doors to the Heatherfield Observatory opened as the automated lock gave way. Then Irma followed Will, Taranee, Cornelia, and Hay Lin across the dark threshold and into the lobby.

*Zzzzsss! Zzzss! Zzzzsssss!*

Irma jumped, hearing the loud bursts of static echoing through the vast marble space. "What was that?" she whispered.

"It's the alarm system," Will said. She walked over to a small control panel on a wall beside the doorway. The static was coming from a speaker within the panel.

"Come right in," the alarm said as Will drew near, "but don't damage anything, or you'll have to answer to me."

"Don't worry, Alarm System," Will replied. "We'll be careful."

Irma shuddered. The whole idea of conversing with machines still freaked her out. Not that her own Guardian abilities were typical for a middle-school girl. Even without the Heart to magnify her powers, Irma could still make bathwater dance, crash ocean waves wherever she wanted to, and redirect rain.

So, okay, Irma conceded to herself: maybe my power over water would freak out a typical kid at Sheffield. But it's certainly not as weird as having a conversation with a home appliance!

"Talking to machines," Irma said aloud. "*There's* something I'll never get used to."

Will smiled. "Are you kidding? Of all my powers, that's my favorite."

Irma couldn't imagine why. For one thing, the appliances Will talked to in her house didn't just make conversation, they actually had *attitude*. Her refrigerator scolded her for eating junk food. Her computer complained about working all the time, and her television set argued with her over what shows she wanted to watch!

"It's really dark in here," Hay Lin whispered.

"You're right," Cornelia said.

Irma glanced around the vast, shadowy lobby. "This place is creepy after hours," she said.

Will shot Irma a look that said, *Chill out, already!*

Irma frowned in reply. Well it is! she thought.

"Taranee, can you help us out?" Hay Lin asked.

"I guess," Taranee replied.

Irma could hear the reluctant tone in Taranee's voice, and it didn't surprise her. The fire Guardian had been griping about this mission ever since they'd rendezvoused at the entrance of Heatherfield Park twenty minutes earlier.

I honestly can't blame her, Irma thought. Professor Lyndon told us there was no Star of Cassidy. So what are we here to see? Nothing!

But Will had insisted that they come there and take a look at the sky for themselves. So, like the rest of the Guardians, Irma had created an astral drop of herself. She had left her magical double behind in her bedroom to keep her parents from realizing she'd gone out. Then she'd bundled up against the chilly night, slipped out of the house, and met the other members of W.I.T.C.H. at the park's entrance. Together they'd trudged through Heatherfield Park and up the observatory steps.

Just like Taranee, however, Irma wasn't too keen on the night's little mission. For one thing, that little peek through the observatory telescope involved some major trespassing. Irma's police-sergeant dad had forgiven her for a lot of bad behavior over the years, but Irma was fairly sure he'd be miffed about the whole breaking-and-entering thing.

Of course, with Will's coaxing the alarm to deactivate on its own, she thought, I *could* make an argument that this is technically just *entering*.

"That's much better!" Hay Lin exclaimed.

Taranee had made a small bright flame appear in her palm. And Irma could finally make out the features of the lobby. Except for the space's being shrouded in shadow, it looked no different from the way it had when they'd been there only a few hours before. There was a cool image of a compass etched into the marble floor, some majestic-looking ivory columns, and a flight of marble steps at the other end of the lobby.

The girls moved slowly toward the staircase. Since Taranee provided the only source of light, she led the way. Like a human torch, she held her fiery palm high. The flickering light cast ghostly shadows across the cold, white marble.

Irma shivered. The whole scene reminded her of the time they'd slipped into the Heatherfield Museum after hours. They'd gone there to find a portal to Metamoor and ended up trapped inside a painting!

"First the museum, and now the observatory," she complained. "We should try sneaking into a bank one of these days!"

Cornelia laughed. "Not one where my pop works, if you don't mind."

"Guys," Taranee said as she continued up

the steps, "are we sure about what we're doing?"

Hay Lin exhaled impatiently. "It's a bit too late to have second thoughts, Taranee. We're already inside!"

Irma rolled her eyes.

I'm with Taranee, she thought, but I'm not saying another word. The others will just jump down my throat.

The girls continued to climb in silence. Up the marble staircase—one floor, then another—they went. Irma couldn't believe that her poor, tired legs had been forced into two StairMaster workouts in the same day!

"Here we go," Irma mumbled under her breath. "Another climb up Everest."

"What was that?" Cornelia asked.

Irma waved her hand. "Nothing," she said, then muttered, "You'd think the least this place could do is provide a Sherpa!"

Several flights further up, the marble steps ended, forcing the girls to switch over to a narrow set of spiral stairs that continued northward. Up, up, up, they climbed.

Just like the last time, Irma griped to herself. The fun never ends!

Finally, the girls reached the door to Professor Lyndon's office. Will whispered a few words to the lock, and it clicked open for her.

Wish I could master *that* trick, Irma thought. On the other hand, there was really no need to as long as Will was leading the way. Irma smiled. She knew that that was one of the great things about being a part of W.I.T.C.H. Each Guardian brought her own totally unique talents to the party.

Irma followed Will, Hay Lin, Cornelia, and Taranee through the professor's office. They crossed to the part of the room with the huge domed ceiling. Taranee held her palm higher, and the burning flame illuminated the massive gray mechanics of the telescope, which sat on a raised platform directly beneath the dome.

Irma checked her watch. They'd been gone from their homes over an hour already. "I just hope our astral drops behave themselves," she said. "It'd be difficult to explain being out this late to my folks."

Hay Lin waved her hand. "Don't worry, our doubles are getting better and better."

I certainly hope so, Irma thought.

She remembered the time Will's astral drop

had slapped Matt Olsen across the face for kissing her. Will had come back from Metamoor to discover that her magical double had gotten into an argument with the boy she had a crush on!

But nothing, *absolutely nothing*, compares to the horror that my own astral drop put me through, Irma thought.

She shuddered at the memory. She'd come back from a harrowing trip to Metamoor to find out from her mother that her astral drop had made a date with Martin Tubbs!

Goofy and skinny, with shaggy hair and Coke-bottle glasses, Martin was not—*repeat, not!*—boyfriend material, as far as Irma was concerned. That hadn't stopped him from waggling his eyebrow at her every chance he got, calling her "sweet thing," or salivating near her locker. *Yuck!*

Irma's astral drop had totally messed up by making that date with Martin. But her mother hadn't let her break the date. So she'd been force to accompany Prince Geek to the Heatherfield Museum. In the end, she'd told Martin to chill, and made sure he understood that the "just friends, not boyfriend" thing was no joke. Thankfully, he'd been cool about the whole thing.

Actually, Irma thought, in the greater scheme of things, the date with Martin hadn't been nearly as bad as the Andrew Hornby incident.

Back when she'd first become aware of her powers, which now seemed like a lifetime ago, Irma had done something very bad.

First, she'd transformed into her Guardian self. Her chunky legs had grown long and lean. She'd sprouted to a willowy height, and her shape had grown curvy. The Guardian Irma was a total hottie, with big, blue, long-lashed eyes and sleek, silky hair. She'd thrown a shawl around her shoulders to hide her wings and snuck out of the house.

Irma had spent the entire night at a cool club called Zot. That was where she'd met up with Andrew, an older boy she'd been trying to talk to forever at school. Andrew was totally cute, but he'd never paid any attention to Irma before. Well, in her gorgeous Guardian form, things had totally changed!

Andrew had talked to her all night. But when he'd offered her a ride home, he'd turned into a real jerk. He'd parked the car in a dark place and completely transformed *him*self: one minute he was boyfriend material and the next he was this leering, obnoxious guy. Irma's reaction had been automatic. Without thinking, she'd caused Andrew to be transformed yet again—into a toad!

*BRRRRRRZZZZZZ!*

The abrupt mechanical noise pulled Irma back from her thoughts. She looked up to find Will sitting in Professor Lyndon's red swivel chair, right in front of the massive telescope.

"And now for a look at the night sky!" Will cried excitedly.

Irma stepped closer and saw that Will had pushed a big blue button that said: OPEN. The machine responded by cranking open the domed roof high above them. Will stood up from the chair and craned her neck to look at the stars.

"Let's hope the telescope stayed on the same coordinates that Professor Lyndon punched in earlier today," she said.

For a long minute, Will just stood there, gazing up at the flickering constellations. The bright moonlight played over her red hair with dancing silver light, and the room went ultra-quiet for several long moments.

Hay Lin exchanged a worried glance with Cornelia. Will seemed to be lost in thought, and nobody quite knew what to say to her. Certainly, their Keeper had gone through a harrowing time, what with losing the Heart and having to fight Nerissa. Irma knew that all of the Guardians were worried about their friend.

Finally, Cornelia stepped up. "Will? What are you hoping to find?" she asked softly.

Will blinked, as if Cornelia's voice had pulled her back from the far corners of space itself. "I'm just following a hunch," she replied. "And, given the situation we're in, I think it's worth a shot."

Will walked back over to the telescope and sat down in the red swivel chair in front of the viewfinder. "Even if the professor didn't see anything," she continued, "that doesn't mean there's nothing to see up there."

Still holding the flame aloft, Taranee sighed with the skepticism of an advanced student in science. "Talking in riddles, now?" she asked. "You sound like the Oracle!"

"All I mean is that the message was intended

for us," Will argued, swiveling the chair around to face her. "And not for anyone else. The name of Cassidy doesn't mean a thing to Professor Lyndon, but it's different for us."

Will swiveled back again, toward the telescope. Irma stepped up with the others, and they formed a close semicircle behind Will.

Okay, Irma thought, we're here for you, Will. We've got your back. Do what you came here to do.

Everyone waited and watched as Will took a deep breath and bent over the viewfinder. Her shaggy red hair fell forward, framing her small, pale face.

For a few moments, Irma held her breath, wondering what Will was looking at so intently. Wow, Irma thought, whatever Will sees must really be something. She's totally into it.

Will remained dead silent. She didn't move. She barely breathed. Irma leaned in, trying to see into the viewfinder for herself. But it was impossible. Only one person at a time could look through the telescope.

With a sigh, Irma leaned back again. After a short while, however, she just could not wait another minute. "Well?" she asked loudly.

Will stiffened.

"Will?" Cornelia prompted.

Leaning back from the viewfinder, Will whispered, "It's—it's incredible, guys." Her brown eyes were wide with amazement.

"What did you see?" Hay Lin asked, leaning forward.

Will stood up from the chair. "Look for your-selves," she said, her eyes still glowing with awe.

The Guardians exchanged nervous glances.

"I'll go first," Irma said, sitting down in the chair.

The viewfinder consisted of an oval-shaped lens about the size of a pair of binoculars. Irma leaned forward, toward the lower half of the tel-escope, and put her eyes as close to the viewing lens as the device would allow.

I can hardly wait to see the great Star of Cassidy, she thought. It must really be something!

Immediately, the night sky lit up for her. She could see a sprinkling of bright stars against the ink-stained canvas of space. She blinked, try-ing to figure out what it was that Will had seen that was so "incredible."

Irma was no genius when it came to astronomy, but she knew enough to know that she was simply looking at a regular old spread of stars that were all about the same size. And all of them appeared to be a part of a typical night-sky constellation.

Irma sighed. Of course, there's no star, she thought. That's what the professor had said, right? We all ended up tramping through a chilly park and watching Will sweet-talk an alarm system for nothing!

Irma leaned back from the viewfinder and sighed again. If they had gone over to Will's house, they could have been eating take-out pizza and watching *Boy Comet* on TV right now. On the other hand, the last time Irma had tried to watch *Boy Comet* on Will's television set, the stupid thing had objected. "My speakers just can't handle it!" the television had complained. Then it had forced them to watch a documentary on the secret life of black bears. *What a bore!*

Still, Irma thought, I would have preferred watching a lame documentary to climbing stairs until my legs were ready to fall off!

"Done?" Hay Lin asked, nudging Irma to move out of the way.

Irma gladly got up from the telescope's seat. She'd seen enough, which is to say, *not much*. "Okay," she said, throwing up her hands. "It's your turn."

Hay Lin sat down and peered into the viewfinder. But after a few seconds of looking, she started to scratch her head in confusion. Finally, she stood up. "I don't see it," she said. "Maybe Taranee should look."

Irma turned to Taranee. "Your turn."

Who knows, Irma thought. Maybe Taranee or Cornelia will see something that Hay Lin and I obviously didn't.

But after a few seconds, Taranee was displaying the same confused reaction that Irma and Hay Lin had.

"*Hmmm,*" Taranee murmured. She leaned back from the viewfinder, took off her large round glasses, and cleaned them with a tissue from her pocket. Then she put them back on again and peered through the viewfinder a second time.

Finally, she shook her head, her single braid flipping from side to side. She glanced worriedly at Cornelia. "It's your turn," she said, rising from the chair.

Cornelia sat down next. Like the others, she appeared not to see anything but a typical dark sky with twinkling stars.

"Well?" Will asked, clearly concerned that no one but she had such an awed reaction.

"*Hmmm . . .*" Cornelia murmured. She looked through the viewfinder again, then leaned back and met Will's eyes. "I'm sorry," she said gently, "but I don't see anything, either."

"That's impossible!" Will cried, throwing up her hands. "I'm not hallucinating. It's right there!"

Irma was now officially worried about Will. The girl claimed to have seen something "incredible." But none of the other Guardians had seen anything out of the ordinary when they had looked through the telescope.

Cornelia got up from the chair. She glanced at everyone's nervous faces. "Maybe we'd better go back home, Will," she said. "It's really late."

Will shook her shaggy red mop and stood her ground under the dome of the observatory.

"You guys, go, if you want to," she said, craning her neck to look up at the night sky. The look on her face was one of determined resoluteness. "I'm staying here. I'll spend the whole night if I have to. But I'm certainly not going to turn back now!"

# EIGHT

The chilly evening air had made everything clearer. There were no clouds that night, nothing to block the moon's glow. Its light appeared to be painting the whole world silver.

Standing below the great open dome of the Heatherfield Observatory, Will almost felt as if she could reach up and slap the craggy white surface of the moon's bright face. Just like my astral drop slapped Matt that time, she mused.

The stars, too, seemed really close that night, Will realized. And now that all her friends had looked through the telescope and seen nothing, she knew that the brightest, most incredible star in the sky that night was shining for her eyes alone.

*But why?* Will thought in frustration. What does it mean? What does any of it mean?

The moon and stars appeared clear enough to Will, but nothing else did. Searching for answers, her mind quickly replayed everything that had brought her to that moment, all the strange events of the last few weeks: the attacks by Nerissa; the increasing burden of the Heart; even that disturbing trip back to Fadden Hills, where she'd met Kadma. . . .

In her mind, Will could still see the old Guardian's almond-shaped eyes, her lovely purple gown, and her long dark braid, heavily threaded with gray. Kadma's eyebrows were gray, too. But her skin looked flawless, with only the faintest trace of wrinkles at the edges of her eyes and mouth.

The old Guardian seemed so elegant, poised, and dignified the day Will had gone back to her old hometown to meet her. But Will knew that Kadma's history had been a terrible one. Kadma had served as a Guardian with Halinor and Yan Lin (Hay Lin's grandmother). The other Guardians in that ancient Power of Five were Nerissa and Cassidy.

After Nerissa had murdered Cassidy,

Kadma and Halinor had been outraged. They'd gone up to Candracar and lashed out at the Oracle. In their view, the Oracle was supposed to be a wise seer. Kadma and Halinor had demanded to know why he could not have foreseen Cassidy's murder. After all, the Oracle himself had given Cassidy the Heart. And that was why Nerissa had betrayed and killed her.

Will still didn't know what to think of it all. Why hadn't the Oracle been able to foresee what his act would have wrought? she now found herself wondering. Or if he had, how could he have let it happen?

One thing Will knew for certain from Kadma's past—the Oracle would not abide being questioned. He'd banished Kadma and Halinor from Candracar. For many years afterward, the two Guardians had lived together on the earth. They'd started the Rising Star Foundation, an orphanage for children without homes and families. Then Halinor had passed away, and Kadma finally revealed some unsettling news to Will: through people they had helped at the orphanage, Halinor and Kadma had been spying on Will for years. Dozens of people Will had known in Fadden Hills—

babysitters, neighbors, and teachers—had been secretly watching over her and reporting back to Halinor and Kadma on her progress.

It was Kadma who had given Will the mysterious leather-bound diary filled with the planets, stars, and constellations. She'd told Will that Halinor had wanted her to have it.

But what good is it? Will thought in frustration, as she continued to gaze at the night sky through the dome of the observatory. I can't read the diary. And I still don't know what seeing the Star of Cassidy really means!

Just then, the star Will had been watching began to grow bigger and brighter. Will didn't think that was possible, but the star actually seemed to be descending toward the earth.

Will's jaw went slack. "Whoa," she whispered.

As the star bathed her in its brilliant beams of crystalline light, Will suddenly remembered what Kadma had told her the day she'd given her the leather-bound diary: *You were born under a lucky star. The Star of Cassidy.*

A voice, clear as crystal, suddenly spoke from somewhere above. "We meet at last, Will."

Will shivered. She didn't just hear the bright

voice, she also felt it, like a cool wind spiraling around her body. But it wasn't a howling, angry gust. The voice she heard was more of a whispering breeze, like a swirling current that refreshes the earth by sweeping down from the highest reaches of the atmosphere.

Will cleared the nervous lump from her throat and rasped, "Is it . . . is it really you?"

"Yes, my friend," the voice replied, with obvious joy and affection. "I've waited so long for this moment!"

That was when it happened. The burning Star of Cassidy descended right from the sky. Down it came, lower and lower, its dazzling brightness increasing until it breached the observatory dome and landed right in front of Will.

"Ah!" Will cried, raising her arms to protect her eyes. The starlight was blinding now, like the Heart of Candracar's blazing energy multiplied by a thousand.

Vaguely, Will was aware of the shouts coming from behind her. Will's best friends were watching her in confusion and alarm.

"Will," Irma called loudly, "have you gone out of your mind? Who are you talking to?"

"Wait!" Cornelia cried, pulling Irma back. "Don't get near her!"

Will heard Irma's and Cornelia's voices, but she didn't dare turn around, for she didn't dare risk letting the Star out of her sight.

"It was an endless wait," the blinding Star told Will, "but for this moment of happiness, I'd go through that silence and loneliness all over again!"

The blinding blaze eased off in that moment, and Will's eyes adjusted to the vision before her.

Oh, my gosh, Will realized, there's a *woman* standing in the light!

She was beautiful, with long, straight hair, some of which had been twisted around her head like a crown. She wore striped Guardian tights and a long, flowing skirt, and her back displayed delicate wings.

Strangely, the woman appeared to be totally colorless. Her form appeared ghostly white, as if she were transparent, and as if fashioned completely of crystal, like the Heart of Candracar; a brilliant sun seemed to be burning deep inside her. Will blinked in stunned awe, unsure of what she should say or do.

"Destiny, fate, or some other mysterious force has seen to it that you were born under my lucky Star, Will," the ghostly woman told her. "And when I was up there and saw you coming, I understood that you were the chosen one."

It was then that Will knew for sure who was standing before her. Without a doubt, she finally knew to whom she was speaking.

"Cassidy!" Will cried.

This is my chance, Will realized, her eyes filling with tears. My chance of a lifetime to speak to another Keeper. My chance to tell her how hard it's been, how terribly I've failed, and to ask if it's really too late to make things right again.

# NINE

Taranee gaped in complete confusion at Will. The girl stood beside the observatory's massive telescope. Her pale face was turned toward the night sky. Her lips were moving, and she was speaking. But she wasn't talking to any of the other Guardians. She was talking to someone Taranee couldn't see—someone only *Will* could see.

This makes no logical sense, Taranee thought. *Unless* . . . it's not supposed to make sense . . .

That was when Will cried out, "Cassidy!"

With wide eyes, Taranee turned to Cornelia, Irma, and Hay Lin. "Hear that?" she whispered, gesturing to Will. "She's—

she's talking to *Cassidy*."

A moment later, Will was sobbing. Tears rolled down her cheeks.

Han Lin gasped and pointed. "Will's *crying*!"

Suddenly Irma sniffed, then wiped a tear away. "It . . . It makes me want to cry, too," she said.

Taranee felt her own eyes misting. Yet she had no reason to feel particularly sad—unless some mysterious force was in the room, making her feel that way.

"Don't you get it?" Irma said. "There's a ghost in the room."

Taranee had come to the same conclusion. An ethereal presence had entered the observatory—the ghost of Cassidy. Clearly, Will was the only one who saw her. But Taranee and the others could actually feel the long-lost Guardian's presence in their heightened emotions.

Before Taranee could speak, however, *another* presence made itself known—and not so quietly.

*KA-RASHHH!*

The girls jumped in surprise when the door

to Professor Lyndon's office came crashing down. Taranee heard an angry snarl and looked up to see a familiar, unfriendly face . . . Khor's!

"There's not just a ghost in the room!" Taranee cried to Hay Lin. "Now there's our old monster friend, too! Man, what a *night*!"

Eyes fiery with savage rage, Khor stared at them, constantly clenching and unclenching his clawed fists. The creature seemed to pause inside the door, as if listening to a faraway voice. Taranee guessed it was Nerissa's. So did Irma.

"That's Nerissa's servant," Irma whispered. "She's probably issuing orders to him right now. And I'm willing to bet none of those orders are coming with a side of french fries!"

Upon seeing Khor that close, Taranee couldn't help getting a flashback to those mythical gods of ancient Egypt she'd studied in history class. The Egyptian gods were represented with human arms, legs, and torsos, but they had animal's heads.

One god in particular popped into Taranee's mind—Anubis. He had the head of a jackal. She thought Khor looked kind of jackal-like, with his beady eyes and slobbering mouth. But one thing was for sure—he hadn't come out of any history book!

Suddenly Khor dropped into a fighting crouch. With a roar, the creature reached into his belt and pulled two stubby swords free.

Taranee heard the blades swish as the monster slashed the air. Then Khor lumbered forward, toward the cowering girls.

"What do we do now?" said Irma. "Without the Heart of Candracar we're short on tricks."

Cornelia thrust her chin out and threw her arms forward. Her blond hair billowed like a veil. "We can't transform!" she cried, "but even if they're weak, we do still have our powers!"

With that, a bolt of raw earth energy crackled from Cornelia's hands. The observatory flashed bright green as the magical lightning struck Khor in the chest.

*RRRAARGH!*

The monster howled. Then he stumbled back, his hairy chest bruised by Cornelia's attack.

You go, earth girl! Taranee thought. But I can't let Cornelia do all the fighting!

Taranee quickly glanced across the room to check on Will. The girl was still transfixed. As she continued to speak with the ghost of Cassidy, she remained completely oblivious to the chaos and danger around her.

Taranee knew that Will would be in real trouble if Khor decided to attack her now. Already the creature was rising again, teeth gnashing, blades clutched in both hairy fists.

"We've got to work together to keep Khor away from Will," Cornelia declared. "We can't let Will's link with Cassidy be broken!"

Taranee knew that Cornelia was right. She thrust her chin forward, face determined. "Let's get to work!" she cried.

Focusing intently, Taranee used her affinity with fire to conjure up a tiny blaze in the palms of her hands. She stared into the crimson glow, willing the flame to increase its size. Without the Heart of Candracar and its power, however, the fire in her hands remained small and weak.

If only I had my full powers! Taranee thought, shaking her head as she remembered how she'd once shunned her mystical abilities. In fact, once upon a time, Taranee had been afraid of fire. But not anymore! Now the girl who had once been nervous about using her skills was all too ready to turn up the heat!

Feeling the blaze begin to swell a little more, Taranee concentrated. Without her full power, she knew that the way to get Khor was through strategy, not strength.

She cupped her hands together until it appeared as if she had already smothered the flame. But it was only a ploy to draw Khor closer. As the beast lunged forward, Taranee opened her hands wide to reveal the small ball of white-hot fire. She ordered the flames to leap from her palms and engulf Nerissa's creature.

Khor roared as the fire struck him. It wasn't enough to defeat him, not by a long shot. But Taranee wasn't finished yet!

"Feel like taking a little trip, pal?" Taranee asked as she followed her fireball surprise with a stream of molten energy. The crackling orange bolts flowed from her fingertips like water from a fire hose.

"*Rrraaargh!*" Khor raged.

Taranee's stinging stream made Khor angry, but it failed to send him running. Taranee's magic alone wasn't enough to move him out of the professor's office—and away from Will and the ghost of Cassidy.

Cornelia stepped up. She lifted her arms. Now the earth Guardian was adding her crackling green stream to Taranee's fiery orange one.

Hay Lin and Irma joined in, too. The air Guardian sent white magic Khor's way. And the water Guardian added her own blue waves.

The monster Nerissa had sent to destroy them was powerful. And the four Guardians were not wielding anything close to their full magical strength. But even Khor could not withstand the blazing assault launched by all of the Guardians at once.

Thrown backward, the monster fell through the professor's office doorway. He rolled down the narrow spiral staircase, flames still licking his body.

Good, Taranee thought. Now Khor can't endanger Will.

But the monster still had to be stopped!

Taranee took off running, following the tumbling monster all the way down to the marble lobby of the observatory. Irma, Hay Lin, and Cornelia followed close behind.

For a few minutes, Taranee was relieved that they had Khor on the run. But when she reached the lobby, she was surprised to find it empty. There was no sign of Khor, no indication he'd been there.

Irma, Hay Lin, and Cornelia arrived a few moments after Taranee. All of them searched around the security desk, then behind the columns that dominated the entranceway.

Weird, Taranee thought. "I'm checking down here!" she called to the others. Then she jogged down one of the long corridors that led from the lobby.

I couldn't have imagined the whole attack, could I? Taranee wondered as she raced along the marble hallway. Nerissa's played tricks on us before—but in our dreams, not during our waking hours.

After a few minutes of searching, Taranee heard a distant roar. "Uh-oh," she murmured, freezing in her tracks.

She turned and ran back toward the lobby. On the way, she heard her friends shouting in panic. But the shouts weren't coming from the lobby. They were echoing up from the observatory's basement.

I've got to find my friends and save them from that monster! Taranee thought.

She yanked open the door to the basement.

The stairwell wasn't like the main observatory; no more pristine white marble. Now she'd have to navigate her way down a dimly lit shaft lined by dirty bricks. A naked bulb hanging from the ceiling was the only source of light. She moved down the rickety wooden staircase and was about to push open the steel basement door when rough claws seized her from the shadows. Taranee struggled, but Khor held her tightly.

"*Ow!*" Taranee screamed.

Khor snarled again. Taranee was helpless in his deadly grip. She longed to transform, to regain her full powers as a Guardian and show this monster what she and her fellow Guardians were *really* made of. But without the Heart, there was nothing she could do.

Struggling helplessly, Taranee watched Khor kick open the steel door. She blinked against the multicolored glow of floating stars, moons, and planets. Taranee recognized the place immediately. Hay Lin and Will had told her about it after their first trip to the observatory.

This was Professor Lyndon's new planetarium. The room was dark, like space. Hidden projectors re-created three-dimensional stars, comets, and asteroids all around. High above, large metal globes of different colors hung from wires to represent the sun and its planets.

*It really does make you feel as if you were walking in space,* she thought.

Taranee realized something else, too. Her friends had been thrown in there by Khor already—that was how they had gotten down there. Cornelia was already rising from the concrete floor. But Irma and Hay Lin didn't look so good. Irma was on the floor, holding her head. And Hay Lin lay face down, motionless.

Just then, Khor hurled Taranee into the massive space. Taranee landed hard near Irma, but quickly scrambled to her feet, then moved to help Irma get back up too.

"Everything okay?" Taranee asked.

"Just great," Irma replied. "Can't you tell?"

"*NNNRRRRRR,*" snarled Khor.

Irma sighed. "And things can only get better."

The creature's mammoth silhouette filled the doorframe. He regarded the girls through angry eyes. Then he lifted a blade and shook it threateningly in their faces.

Taranee knew they had to act quickly. "Let's split up!" she cried. "The monster's ready to attack again!"

Roaring in triumph, Khor charged in to the chamber. As the girls scattered, Irma stumbled and fell under the heavy, glowing model of the sun, dangling from the ceiling on a thin wire.

The creature, seeing the girl under the orb, hurled his glistening blade. Like a boomerang the razor-sharp sword cut through the air—and right through the wire holding the model.

"Look out, Irma!" Taranee cried.

The wire snapped with a *ping*, and the heavy globe plunged down.

# TEN

Will's eyes, meanwhile, remained wide and awestruck. Her attention continued to stay fixed on the visiting Star of Cassidy.

"What's going on?" Will asked, putting a hand to her woozy head.

Cassidy's ghostly presence was so powerful, so emotional, that it was almost overwhelming. But Will had sensed that something else was disturbing her. A heavy gloom was now present in the observatory.

"Everything's fine, Will," Cassidy said. "Nerissa's darkness has reached this place, but it can do nothing against the power of light . . . nor against your friends' bravery." Cassidy closed her eyes. "Your friends are protecting you."

*What?* Will tried to shake her fuzzy head clear. If her friends were in danger, she couldn't just stand by and do nothing. "I've got to help them!" Will cried.

But before Will could dash away, Cassidy reached out her ghostly hand and closed her glowing white fingers around Will's wrist. Will tried to break free, but the power of light held her firmly in place.

"Let me go, Cassidy!" she cried.

"No, Will. You have to listen to me. Our contact won't last much longer, and your friends will manage, even without you, you'll see."

Will didn't know whether to believe Cassidy or not.

"You were great at understanding the message in my diary," Cassidy continued. "Our meeting took place at the only possible moment. . . ."

"The *worst* possible moment," Will said, correcting her and gritting her teeth. It had been the moment of her complete and utter failure as Keeper of the Heart! Will shook her head. "I've lost the Heart of Candracar," she confessed to Cassidy. "I gave it to Nerissa." Her shoulders slumped. She hung her head. A tear slipped down her cheek. Just the act of saying that out loud had taken something out of her. "Now she will destroy the Temple, and it will be my fault!"

Cassidy moved closer to Will and rested a reassuring hand on her small shoulder. "I know all about it, Will," she whispered, "and you shouldn't blame yourself."

"How can you say that?" Will turned away in shame from the former Keeper. "I messed up, Cassidy. I've been a total failure."

"You're the best Keeper of the Heart there's ever been," Cassidy insisted. "You're destined to do great things, and soon you'll discover that."

"You talk like the Oracle!" Will's impatience was rising now. The tremendous burden of the Heart had weighed heavily on her since Nerissa's return. Day in and day out, Will had tried to be true to her responsibility as Keeper, but it hadn't been easy. In fact it had been totally exhausting. And, in the end, she'd been tricked into giving the Heart away. So how could Cassidy say those things?

Will turned on the ghost. "If you know

something, you've got to tell me. Please, Cassidy . . . I'm sick of living like this!"

Cassidy looked up with reverence at the sky, as if she were peering into Candracar itself. "Before Nerissa did away with me, the last thing I thought of was the Oracle."

Will blinked. "You did?"

Cassidy nodded. "At that moment, I hated him with every fiber of my being. Even more than I hated Nerissa."

"You hated the Oracle?" Will whispered, shocked that Cassidy would admit something like that.

"But then I understood," Cassidy said.

Will furrowed her brow in confusion. "What? What did you understand?"

"The Oracle and Nerissa," Cassidy replied. "They had each done exactly what they were supposed to, according to their own nature. Will, without them, without me, you would never be where you are now."

"But the Oracle let Nerissa destroy you," Will argued. "Where's the justice in that?"

"Nerissa and I were instruments of balance," Cassidy explained. "I feel no ill will for her . . . only gratitude."

"Gratitude?" Will whispered. "But how? Why?"

"Achieving balance in the worlds watched over by Candracar often involves making difficult, unbearable decisions," Cassidy said, "but these actions cannot be viewed or judged from one person's perspective."

Cassidy stepped closer to Will. She placed both hands on Will's shoulders now, and peered into her wide brown eyes. "Beyond the skies of Candracar lies chaos. Will, compared to that chaos, every danger you've encountered so far is nothing."

Will swallowed uneasily. With the loss of the Heart, she didn't know what she could do to save the universe from chaos. "Why are you telling me all this, Cassidy?" she asked.

"So that the idea of giving up or giving in never crosses your mind," Cassidy replied. "Always remember the five ancient Guardians. Each one, in her own way, contributed to your growth. You're tenacious, and up until now you've always faced your commitments with responsibility. But in the future, always remember this moment."

Will worriedly rubbed her forehead. This

was all so much to take in . . . to understand and believe. "But what task is in store for me, Cassidy?" she asked. "What will my future be?"

Cassidy closed her eyes and smiled, as if she were tapping into the cosmic forces of the universe. Gradually, Will felt a sweet warmth drift over her, like a soft blanket. It calmed her, filling her with an overwhelming sense of peace.

Cassidy's eyelids fluttered; then her gaze met Will's. "Your future will hold many challenges," Cassidy said, "which is why I'm giving you my spark, and with it my Heart."

Like a lily spreading its petals, Cassidy extended her ghostly white fist and opened it. Hovering above the old Keeper's glowing palm was an exact copy of the Heart of Candracar. The crystal shined as brightly as a sun, nearly blinding Will with its radiant energy.

Awestruck, Will watched Cassidy's dazzling Heart float slowly toward her. She reached out with trembling hands to draw it in. Cassidy smiled, seeing Will recover what she thought she'd lost.

"Good-bye, Will!" the ghostly ex-Keeper called, ascending slowly toward the opening in the observatory's domed ceiling. "Our paths must part, but I'll continue to watch over you from afar. Nothing disappears forever. Things often just change form, and someday . . . we'll be together once again."

In amazement, Will watched as Cassidy's transparent silhouette slowly dissolved back into the brilliant, dazzling starlight. Then the starlight continued its rise, farther and farther above the horizon, until finally it reclaimed its place in the firmament.

"Thank you, Cassidy!" Will called, sending her voice skyward. She looked down at the Heart in her hand, then back up at the constellations once more. But the Star of Cassidy was gone! The glow had faded into the night until it had disappeared. Suddenly, Will knew why. Its light was now shining somewhere else.

In her palm, Cassidy's Heart continued to send out rays of brilliant energy. Will could feel the extraordinary power pulsing from its very core.

"This is incredible," Will whispered. "More than I could have ever hoped for."

Just then, Will heard a terrible roar from somewhere inside the observatory. She looked around. But Irma, Taranee, Cornelia, and Hay Lin were nowhere in sight. A second later, Will heard their shouts and cries echoing up from the stairwell. Will's best friends were in trouble. They needed her help.

With renewed determination, Will narrowed her eyes as she gazed at the blazing gift in her palm. "Now all I have to do," she whispered, "is find out if this copy of the Heart works like the original."

# ELEVEN

*GUR-RAAAAAARGH!*

Vaguely, as if from a distance, Hay Lin heard Khor's angry snarl. She felt someone tug her arm. Opening her eyes, she found herself lying on a cold stone floor. She rolled onto her back and saw colorful planets, moons, stars, and comets floating over her head.

Just then, she heard a shout. "Look out, Irma!"

With a crash, a large model of the sun smashed to the ground and toward Irma. The water Guardian rolled across the floor just in time. The heavy orb had missed her by mere inches!

Hay Lin's arm was soon being tugged at again. She blinked and found herself looking up to see Cornelia. The girl knelt over her, a worried expression on her pretty face.

"Are you . . . are you all in one piece?" Cornelia asked.

Hay Lin sat up and rubbed the back of her head. "I . . . I think so," she moaned, checking her arms and legs. "I ache all over, but I don't think anything's broken."

Relief flowed over Cornelia's features. Then her expression turned steely. "Pick yourself up, and let's get moving!" she sharply commanded. "The game's not over yet!"

Sitting in the corner, Irma kicked debris out of her way and pushed back her hair, which had fallen over her face. "I don't know about you guys," she called, "but I'd settle for a tied score!"

*RAAAAARGH!*

In the center of the room, Khor batted aside a model of a red planet. The wire holding it to the ceiling snapped and sent the globe rumbling into a corner, where it was smashed to bits. The sword-wielding hulk threw back his head and roared again.

"Come on!" Cornelia cried to Hay Lin. "Let's go!"

Whoa, Hay Lin thought, Cornelia sure has been taking charge a lot lately—which is actually fine with me. After all, *somebody's* got to do it, since Will lost the Heart.

Unfortunately, Hay Lin feared it wouldn't matter who took charge now. Without their Guardian powers and the Heart of Candracar, they didn't have much of a chance for victory. Of course, *survival* alone might be nice, Hay Lin thought.

A few feet away, Taranee sprang forward to help Irma get back up off the ground. "With our powers at their lowest, Khor is too difficult an enemy!" Taranee warned.

But Cornelia remained defiant. "That beast is just trying to scare us!"

Irma rolled her eyes. "Well, he's doing a great job, if you ask me!"

Hay Lin watched the chaos, not sure what to do. For a moment, she wondered if her grandmother had ever been in a situation like this one. Had Yan Lin ever been caught without the power of the Heart in the face of mortal danger?

Truly, this was not an ideal situation, Hay Lin thought, and Grandma *did* warn me once that life was no noodle-salad picnic! On the other hand, she'd never mentioned any specifics—like evil monsters throwing giant planets at you in the basement of your boyfriend's observatory!

Still wobbly, Hay Lin rose to her feet. She kept one eye on Khor and the other on her threatened friends. Just then, the monster snarled, lowered his head, and shook it like a bull.

"He's charging again!" Hay Lin cried.

Unfortunately her warning served only to attract Khor's attention. Ignoring the others, the creature immediately rushed toward Hay Lin.

"*Aaagh!*" Hay Lin squealed.

She whirled, then took off running. Just then, Hay Lin wished more than anything that she could soar through the air. But she knew it was not to be. With the Heart of Candracar under Nerissa's evil control, air girl was currently grounded!

One of Khor's giant paws gripped the long blue-black pigtails dangling down Hay Lin's back. He jerked her to a halt as she squawked. Grunting, Khor yanked her backward.

Helpless to resist, Hay Lin felt the creature's

powerful claws on her neck. She panicked, then tried to thrash, to break away. But he was too strong. And his tight grip on her throat was starting to cut off her air supply.

I'm the air Guardian, she thought frantically. And, boy, do I need some!

With his powerful arm, Khor lifted Hay Lin off her feet. Dangling high in the air, she felt the hot panting of the evil creature on her cheek.

Irma screamed hysterically. "Hey! Hey!"

Cornelia shouted a warning. "Stay back, guys!"

*RRAAAAH!*

Khor's howl battered Hay Lin's ears. Faintly, she heard a moan escape from her own lips. Is this it? Hay Lin wondered. Have we finally been defeated?

"Hah!" Irma cried. "Like I'm going to stand around and watch this!"

Through a dizzy haze, Hay Lin saw Irma charge the monster. Her friend began to pummel the creature's broad back with her tiny fists.

"Let go of her right now, you beast!" Irma screamed. "Let *go-o-o-o-o-o-o-o*!"

But Khor didn't let go. Instead, Hay Lin felt

his claws tighten even more around her neck until she couldn't breathe at all.

Then suddenly Hay Lin was freed. The pressure on her throat eased, and she felt herself falling to the ground. Someone had attacked Khor with a bolt of energy, loosening his deadly hold.

The monster howled again, and Hay Lin opened her eyes in time to see a second bolt of raw, magical power strike Khor in the back. The monster roared and threw up his clawed hands in fury.

"Didn't you hear what my friend just told you, Khor?" asked a familiar voice.

That was when Hay Lin saw Will—only it wasn't the old Will anymore. Her best friend had changed into her Guardian form, limbs long and strong, head unbowed, eyes burning with knowledge and a fierce resolve. Will literally crackled with mystical power; her wings fluttered around her, beating the air into stormy currents.

"W—Will?" Taranee cried.

Will grinned. "Just in the nick of time, huh?"

Taranee hurried to Will's side. "But . . . if you managed to transform, that means you've got the Heart of Candracar back!"

Will nodded and displayed what looked like the original Heart medallion in her hand. She gazed into the glowing crystal, then closed her fingers around it again.

"Well," she told Taranee, "let's just say it's something that looks a lot like it. It's a gift from Cassidy."

Despite her aches and pains, Hay Lin nearly whooped for joy. Make way for air girl, she thought, 'cause she's making a flying comeback!

"I'll explain it all to you later on," Will quickly told the others. "Right now, let's get the show on the road!"

Raising her hand above her head, Will opened her fist again—and there was Cassidy's Heart. The crystal orb hovered above Will's palm for a moment. Will lifted her chin, and the entire room began to glow with bright pink energy. Her hair, silky and sleek now, floated around her like a glistening red halo. Then the pulsing core of the Heart exploded, and blinding rays flashed through the observatory basement, engulfing her friends in dazzling energy.

The magical forces whirled around Hay Lin like a tornado, enclosing her in a white teardrop of pulsing light. Hay Lin felt the ancient energy flow through her body, endowing her with power and buoyancy. Her limbs grew longer. Her body grew taller and stronger. Her pigtails brushed against her cheeks as the magical winds whipped them around her maturing face.

Finally Hay Lin's wings—her wonderful, wonderful, purple-and-turquoise wings!—reappeared. She felt them flutter and beat against the air. Joyously, Hay Lin raised her arms as the Power of Five flowed through her. She was a Guardian again!

"Air!" Hay Lin triumphantly cried.

"Water!" Irma cried after her own blue teardrop of mystical energy flowed around her like an ocean whirlpool, transforming her completely.

A burst of green magic corkscrewed around Cornelia's body. As she received the power, her golden hair flew outward, and her eyes danced with electric energy. "Earth!" Cornelia called.

Finally, Taranee's glowing teardrop turned bright red, then fiery orange, as the ancient magic surrounded and suffused her with her elemental power. "Fire!" she shouted.

When their transformations were complete, the Guardians lined up in a row to face the stunned monster. Once again, their radiant, mystical forms had truly become the Power of Five.

*We are powerful.*
*We are magical.*
*We are a united force.*
*We are the Guardians!*

Will put her hands on her hips and smirked at the ugly, hulking creature. "So, Khor, where were we?" she asked.

Khor stared in stunned awe at the transformed girls. He knew he was outmatched. With a terrified howl, he ran out of the planetary chamber and up the narrow, rickety staircase.

Irma giggled. "I didn't get those last few words, but from the tone of his voice, I don't think poor Khor likes our little surprise."

Hay Lin laughed at Irma's joke. She felt like laughing at everything now! Above their heads, the Guardians heard Khor crashing about inside the lobby of the observatory.

"Let's wear him out a bit!" Will cried.

Hay Lin grinned. The Keeper had definitely taken charge of the Guardians again!

"Come on," Will commanded. "Let's go!"

Together, the Guardians raced up the stairs to the lobby. Khor snarled a warning when the girls stumbled upon him. He was trying to escape through the front door.

Unfortunately, Khor couldn't talk to machines or chat with locks the way Will could. And the heavy door was just too tough to break down, even for a mighty monster like Khor.

"There he is!" cried Hay Lin, targeting the monster. She spread her arms and flapped her wings, then soared into the air.

Khor followed me once before, when I shouted a warning to the others, Hay Lin thought. Maybe I can get his attention again.

Like a crazy hummingbird, Hay Lin circled the monster's head several times. She whacked him once or twice, just to provoke him. Khor swatted at her angrily, as if she were a purple-and-turquoise fly. But he couldn't catch her.

Hay Lin was just too fast for him.

"Over here, silly!" Hay Lin called, leading Khor to a tall window overlooking Heatherfield Park. The creature followed the darting Guardian, snatching at air as he tried to drag Hay Lin down.

The other Guardians circled the monster, ready to unleash their phenomenal powers. Poor Khor didn't have a chance, and the creature was starting to figure that out. He reacted like a trapped animal. With a frustrated snarl, the beast hurled one of his curved blades right at Hay Lin!

Oh, no, you don't, Dog Face, Hay Lin thought. She quickly ducked, and the blade thudded into the wall right above her head. Whew! That was close! she thought.

Irma called out to her friend. "Hey, Taranee!" she shouted, her hands crackling with magical energy. "What do you say? Do we light up the grill?"

Taranee grinned. "Sure thing! I love barbecues."

Taranee lifted her arms. Over the girl's head, a firestorm began to brew. First it was a tiny flame. Then the blaze got bigger and bigger.

The hot orange ball continued to swell in size until it was as large as a beach ball.

The heat scorched Hay Lin and the others. They scattered, giving Taranee some space. In mere seconds, the fireball burned so bright that it illuminated the shadowy observatory lobby like the noonday sun. Then, with a final cry, Taranee hurled the blazing ball at Khor.

The ball struck Khor full in the chest with a fiery whoosh. The creature roared in fury as he fell back through the window. Glass shattered with a terrible crash; sharp shards were scattered all over the stone floor. Howling, Khor plunged through the broken frame and down, landing with a thud on the park grass below.

The smell of smoke and singed hair filled the observatory. Cautiously, the Guardians approached the window. Hay Lin felt the cool night air streaming in through the shattered window. She welcomed its clean freshness, hoping it would quickly disperse the stench in the observatory. After all, the wreckage in there was bad enough. What would Eric and his grandfather think in the morning if they caught a whiff of scorched monster?

"What a mess!" Will declared.

"Just think of the repair bill," said Cornelia.

"But where did he go?" Taranee cried, vainly looking for Khor. "He was hit hard, so he couldn't have gotten very far."

But the park below was in shadows. There was no sign of the ugly beast.

"Wait! There he is," Cornelia cried, pointing. "He's down in the bushes, behind those trees."

Together, the Guardians gazed down at the motionless figure of Khor. Suddenly the creature lifted his head and cocked his ears as if listening. Then he sprang to his feet and hurried away across a wide stretch of lawn.

As the Guardians watched, a hole opened up in the middle of the lawn. With a final snarl of rage and defiance, Khor leaped through it. A moment later, the hole closed up and the lawn was smooth again. Khor was gone.

Will sighed. "He must be going back to his friend Nerissa."

"Nerissa again," said Cornelia with a frown.

"Yeah, Nerissa," Will replied. "Cassidy said she'd forgiven her for what she'd done. For me, that'll be impossible."

Cornelia nodded. "How could you? I mean,

just look at what Nerissa has done to us!"

Sitting on the windowsill, Taranee waved the conversation aside. "Let's talk about it some other time." She hopped off the sill and approached the others. "Right now, let's get out of here. Who knows how Eric and the professor will react if they find us here—and see the mess Khor made of the lobby."

Hay Lin sighed. "If I know the professor, he's probably already telling Eric to call the police."

Irma went pale. "My father's got a night shift tonight. Let's get out of here!"

Will nodded. "You're right. Let's get going. But we're not going *home*. Not yet!"

Hay Lin blinked in surprise. "Then where?"

"I think we'd better take a little trip to Candracar," Will replied. "Right now."

# TWELVE

Nerissa was furious! Her blue eyes flashed with rage. Her bone-white teeth gnawed at her blood-red lips. "Why do they vex me so?" she cried. "Why must I deal with those insufferable Guardians *yet again*?"

Nerissa hated to waste energy on those pesky girls from Heatherfield. It was an irritating diversion, especially since she was so close to gaining her revenge on the Oracle and the Congregation of Candracar.

But the Guardians were proving to be unbelievably stubborn. Nerissa had tricked Will into giving her the Heart of Candracar, the very *source* of their Guardian power. Yet the girls still resisted and fought her.

Earlier that day, even without the Heart, that mop-headed waif, Will, had escaped Nerissa's carefully woven dream snare.

Nerissa knew the Guardians were up to something when they'd snuck out of their homes in the dead of night, leaving their astral drops behind. She'd kept one eye on them all along, fearing they'd make some ridiculous attempt to regain their power. Even though her plan for revenge was coming along quite nicely, Nerissa didn't want to leave anything to chance. She had the Oracle right where she wanted him, and she had the Heart of Candracar, but it would have been foolish to underestimate the Guardians. As a former Guardian herself, Nerissa knew that better than anyone.

Then it had happened. The Guardians had gone to the observatory, and the little Keeper had spotted a flicker of hope. The moment Will had looked into that telescope and seen that incredible star, Nerissa had sensed something important . . . an unexpected threat and an unforeseen return.

*No!* Nerissa thought. I'm not about to let anything give those bratty little Guardians hope!

That was why Nerissa had ordered Khor to the observatory. Her savage servant was supposed to have diverted the Guardians' attention from seeking help from the skies above. More than anything else, Nerissa had wanted Khor to rid her of the Guardian threat forever.

With her powerful sorcery, Nerissa had directed Khor like a puppet. She'd told her monster to stalk and destroy the five girls. And she'd thought he'd have an easy time of it, too.

Unfortunately, she'd thought wrong!

Even without their powers, the Guardians had held their own against her blade-wielding beast.

"Still the Guardians fight!" Nerissa had screamed, waking her servant Shagon out of his stupor.

Although his senses had been dulled by Nerissa's powerful, binding spell, Shagon had questioned the possibility of the Guardians' resistance.

"How can it be?" the once-human Shagon had asked. "The Heart of Candracar is in our hands, and the Guardians are a universe away."

His question had only made Nerissa angrier.

"Don't try to contradict me, Shagon!" Nerissa had roared at her favorite servant. "The Guardians haven't been defeated yet. I can feel it."

Why do they fight on when they know it's hopeless? Nerissa wondered. Their refusal to accept defeat vexes me to no end! Stupid, stubborn creatures!

In truth, Nerissa had suspected that more than the Guardians' stubbornness was at play. She'd begun to worry that something powerful might have joined the struggle against her.

"I sense an unexpected threat. An unforeseen return," Nerissa had confided to Shagon. "But whatever it is, I won't let it stop me now!"

That was why she'd sent Khor to deal with the Guardians. Her own focus wasn't on the earth. Her primary concern was the coming battle here in the realm of Candracar.

Unfortunately, Nerissa quickly realized that Khor couldn't handle the job she'd given him. Instead of dealing destruction, Nerissa had watched helplessly as Khor himself was blasted down a set of stairs.

Nerissa gritted her teeth and clenched her

fists, watching her servant's humiliation from another dimension.

"No!" Nerissa howled.

But she could do nothing. Nerissa was forced to watch the Guardians *transform*! Somehow, in some way, they had gotten another Heart! They had magnified and united their Guardian powers and defeated Khor, then tossed him out a window like trash.

"Get up, you flea-bitten monstrosity!" Nerissa commanded. "*Sic 'em,* boy!"

But the worthless monster lay on the grass, unable to move.

Nerissa had to do something! She tapped into Khor's brutish mind with her own, reawakening the unconscious beast.

"Get up, Khor!" she commanded. "Get up and fight. Nerissa orders you to!"

Khor opened his eyes, and Nerissa sensed fear. Khor was afraid of the Guardians!

"Your life means nothing to me!" Nerissa angrily cried. "You have to eliminate them. That's an order—" But her thoughts were interrupted.

"No!" The strong, firm voice came seemingly out of nowhere.

Strong hands seized Nerissa, crushing her arms in a punishing grip. "That's not fair!" Shagon shouted, his blank mask of a face only inches from Nerissa's. "You can't sacrifice Khor to satisfy your childish whim!"

"How dare you!" Nerissa replied, shaking off Shagon's grip.

Nerissa knew, of course, why Shagon was objecting. Unlike her other servants, Shagon had been fashioned from a human shell. Nerissa had given him incredible strength—along with the handy ability to grow stronger when hate and rage were unleashed upon him. But even though Nerissa considered him her most trusted servant, there was one thing about him that she just couldn't stand.

Being human, Shagon had free will, buried deep beneath Nerissa's spell. And, because Khor had once been Shagon's loyal dog, the human being inside him wanted to save his friend from destruction.

"Come back to me, my dear friend," Shagon called, his voice reaching Khor through Nerissa's mental connection.

In her mind, Nerissa saw Khor rise and cross the night-shadowed park with a loping gait. She glared at Shagon, ready to confront him. But he confronted her first.

"We can't lose a warrior like Khor," he said. "When he returns, we can take the fortress by storm."

Shagon, you are so tiresome! she thought.

"I decide what we do!" she cried.

But Shagon was unmoved by her declaration. Nerissa suddenly realized that Shagon was as stubborn as the Guardians. Why were these humans so hard to control?

Her own thoughts were quickly interrupted, however, when Khor's visions entered her mind. Nerissa saw through the brute's feral eyes; she watched as a portal opened and the creature leaped into its preternatural glow.

Shagon was happy now. But Nerissa was not. She could not believe that Khor had abandoned the fight! Nor could she forgive Shagon. He had acted on his own to retrieve his friend, against her express command!

Nerissa felt the need to punish Shagon for his insolence. But a stronger desire instantly overwhelmed that one—her lust for vengeance.

To destroy Candracar, she would need Shagon's help. Now that Will had recovered the power of the Heart, Nerissa's need for strength was never more crucial. So, instead of lashing out in anger at Shagon, something that would have given him even more power against her, Nerissa simply glared at him in silent rage.

I still need you, Shagon! she thought. But you'll pay for your insolence soon. . . . Very soon!

# THIRTEEN

Two Elders brought Caleb his clothing. In the middle of the Temple of Candracar, they helped him don his brown trousers; vest; cape; and thick, heavy boots. Caleb politely thanked them. It felt good to be in his old familiar rebel clothes again.

He had been in such a hurry to barge into the Temple's Great Hall that he'd failed to realize he was improperly dressed. Clad only in the loose white tunic he'd thrown on after emerging from the Cosmos of Abeyance, he'd approached the Oracle without taking the time to retrieve his old clothes. Against tradition and protocol, Caleb had spoken boldly to the seer in front of the entire Congregation.

But Caleb hadn't been able to stop

himself. Since awakening from his long sleep, he felt driven to speak out. He had to be a part of this war, this fight against Nerissa.

To Caleb's surprise, the Oracle had not banished him from the assembly for his rude outburst. Caleb had openly defied the Oracle's wishes. He had insisted he was strong enough to fight. Still, the Oracle allowed Caleb to remain among the Congregation.

As Caleb finished dressing himself, he began to reconsider the Oracle's words. Am I really strong enough? he wondered. He *felt* strong. Somewhere inside of him, his heart was still beating out a rebel cadence. Whatever lived inside of him that had urged him to become a rebel leader on Metamoor was now urging him to fight in this war.

But still, the Oracle's expressed worries stayed with him. And a small part of Caleb felt a whisper of doubt. After suffering terrible wounds battling Nerissa, was he really strong enough to fight her again? And after struggling to regain his memories, had he regained enough of his warrior spirit to prevail against a foe as powerful and ruthless as that vengeful sorceress?

Caleb's worried thoughts were interrupted by the arrival of a captain from the outer walls of the Temple. With reverence and respect, the man approached the Oracle and bowed his head.

"What news do you bring?" the Oracle asked.

"Bad news, Oracle," the captain replied.

Groans of misery and frustration rose up from the ranks of the gathered Elders. The Oracle nodded, silently inviting the man to continue.

"Nerissa is preparing to attack us," the captain warned. "We can see her evil servants from the highest walls."

For a moment, the Oracle absorbed the troubling news. Then he replied, "Return to your place, and don't lose her from view."

"As you wish," the captain replied. He bowed deeply and backed away from the Oracle.

After the man was gone, Yan Lin touched the Oracle's arm and spoke to him. Caleb strained to hear their exchange.

"Are you concerned for the girls?" the Oracle asked.

The *girls*, Caleb repeated to himself. Immediately, he thought of the Guardians—and Cornelia. Could she be in danger? he wondered.

Yan Lin shook her head. "I have no idea where they are."

To Caleb's surprise, the Oracle smiled. "Don't worry, Yan Lin. They are close by."

"Closer than you think!" a bright young voice announced.

It was Will, Caleb realized. He watched the Keeper of the Heart of Candracar stride into the chamber ahead of the other Guardians. He recognized Irma, Taranee, and—

"Hay Lin!" cried Yan Lin with joyful recognition. The revered Elder hurried forward to embrace her granddaughter.

Finally, Caleb's eyes found the vision he'd longed for months to embrace. His heart soared when he spied his beloved earth Guardian. "Cornelia!" he cried. "You're safe!"

"Caleb!" Cornelia called as she rushed forward to greet him. They met in the center of the Temple. First their hands touched, then their arms. Finally their lips met in a loving kiss neither of them wanted to break.

When they finally parted, they gazed into each other's eyes. With a deep, satisfied sigh, Caleb reached out and stroked Cornelia's tear-dappled face, caressed her soft cheek, and ran his hands through her long golden mane.

Caleb knew that the struggle against Nerissa was putting them all in terrible danger. But for this one precious moment, he forgot everything but the cerulean blue of Cornelia's eyes, the warm passion of her touch, the sweet taste of her soft lips.

"I'm dying of happiness," Cornelia said, sighing deeply. Her eyes were closed, and Caleb could feel the electricity in her skin wherever he touched her.

Irma, who'd been watching the happy couple from the sidelines, glanced at her fellow Guardians. "Dying? Now? After everything we've been through?" she quipped with a wink.

His hands tucked into the wide sleeves of his robe, the Oracle greeted the Guardians with a placid nod. His gaze appeared content as he took them all in. Then the Oracle directed his attention to the Keeper of the Heart.

"Will, I hear you've spoken to Cassidy," said the Oracle in his gentle voice.

"That's right, sir," she replied. "We're ready to fight now."

The Oracle frowned and shook his head. "It's not time yet," he warned. Then he said something else, something strange. "Don't you have something to ask me, Will?"

Will met the Oracle's neutral gaze with an expression of puzzlement. "Cassidy explained a lot of things to me, and I wish I had more time to ponder all that she said. But this I know." Will placed her hand over her heart. "The Heart of Candracar is lost, but I can still feel it inside of me."

The Oracle responded with a knowing nod. "You are right, Will. What makes us strong isn't objects, but the resources we have within us."

Just when Caleb had been ready to surrender to his self-doubt, he heard the Oracle's assertion and knew his words could not have been truer. What really mattered in any fight, in any struggle, were those things within oneself. In that moment, Caleb remembered his own steadfast determination, his willingness never to give up. *That*, he realized, was what had driven him for most of his life.

This, more than anything, is my identity, he

thought. This is who I am.

It was Caleb's inner strength that had helped him defeat the evil Prince Phobos. Even during the lowest points in that struggle, Caleb had never succumbed to Phobos's dark and powerful will. And, of course, Caleb knew that his own brave heart and fighting spirit were what had helped him become human in the first place!

Buoyed by that knowledge, Caleb felt great joy. He now felt certain that, even newly awakened from his healing sleep, his fighting heart could still prevail in the coming war!

I *am* ready, Caleb realized. Nerissa is the one who should be feeling fear and doubt now, not me!

Caleb studied Will. He hoped the Keeper had listened to the Oracle as he had. He hoped she had understood. Caleb knew that it was truly the spirit that made one mighty, not weapons.

With Cornelia's arm linked through his, Caleb approached the Oracle and respectfully bowed.

"Please tell us, Oracle. What do we do now?" Caleb asked. "We can't just wait for them to attack. Nerissa and her servants are right outside the walls of Candracar. We have to do something, and do it now!"

The Oracle offered no reply. Caleb searched the chamber for someone who would support his cause, plead his case. Only then did he notice Cornelia's anguish, her fear for his safety.

"You must understand," he whispered to Cornelia, "the fire has been ignited inside of me once again. I am a *warrior*, and no true warrior waits for an enemy to attack if he knows the attack is coming."

He stepped forward to address the citizens of Candracar. "We know Nerissa and her minions are coming. It is time to act!"

# FOURTEEN

Cornelia listened to Caleb speak of war and battles, and her spirit sank. She had yearned to hear tender words from her beautiful boy, murmurs of love, and promises of joyful days to come. But that was not what she got. Fate had again conspired to ruin their happiness.

One brief moment, Cornelia thought. One quick kiss, and then the weight of the world comes crashing down on us again!

"But it doesn't have to be that way," Cornelia murmured to herself.

While Caleb recuperated in the Cosmos of Abeyance, the Oracle had released him from his obligation to serve as the Herald of Candracar. With that heavy burden lifted, Caleb was free to go wherever he wished. But, judging by Caleb's own words, and the burning look in his eyes, he seemed to desire only more strife, more war.

My passion is for Caleb, Cornelia thought sadly. But his passion is obviously for the upcoming struggle against Nerissa.

She silently stood by, watching Caleb argue for quick action against the mounting threat. And it was hard not to admire his fire.

He would fight a lion with his bare hands, she thought. But I wonder . . . how would he deal with Heatherfield?

Cornelia began to imagine a future with Caleb. More than anything she'd *ever* wanted in her entire life, she wanted this. . . .

She visualized the day Caleb would meet her family for the first time—at a Sunday dinner, or maybe a holiday get-together. Cornelia imagined her mother smiling, her father offering a welcoming handshake. They'd have a polite conversation. Caleb would impress everyone, of course. And there'd be a round of happy toasts.

But would that actually happen? Cornelia couldn't help asking herself. What would a magical warrior like Caleb have in common with a bank president, like my father? What would he say to my mom, my little sister, or my grandmother?

If I made him go through all that, would he embrace it? Or would he resent it? Cornelia silently wondered.

And then there was school. Caleb could enroll at Sheffield with her. *How cool would that be?* He could come to the dances with her, sit with her at lunch, hang out with her after school. They could work on class projects together and—

Cornelia's runaway imagination came to an abrupt halt.

Caleb was so tall and strong and *mature* that Cornelia doubted he could even fit in at her school. Obviously, Caleb would have to attend classes at the local high school.

But . . . but then I would hardly see him, she mused. He might as well be back in Candracar!

In high school, Caleb would be a star athlete for sure, Cornelia realized, and popular, too. He would always be busy with high school things. Shop projects. The football team . . . perhaps even a pretty cheerleader?

The thought of Caleb going to classes with all those high school girls cut like a knife through Cornelia's heart!

She often saw high school seniors on the street or at the mall. They were so tall, so together, so shapely and mature looking.

Cornelia was no slouch, but she wasn't kidding herself. Her non-Guardian self was still in middle school, not very shapely, and far less glamorous than her magical persona.

I'd look like a little girl next to Caleb, she began to think . . . and she panicked. And then I'd probably end up feeling like a little girl, too—silly, stupid, naive. How would Caleb feel if he saw me the way I am in my normal life?

Caleb had only seen Cornelia in her Guardian form. He'd never seen her as she really was. He'd never seen the Cornelia who lived with her family in a Heatherfield highrise. He'd never met the Cornelia who went to school at Sheffield Institute with all the other kids.

But for them to be together, Cornelia knew that Caleb would have to accept her in her non-Guardian form. That meant no powers, no gossamer wings, and a real body that was much younger and smaller than the one he'd seen.

Would Caleb accept me like that? Cornelia wondered. Would he still love me like that?

Cornelia recalled the time Irma had decided that she wanted to look absolutely amazing for one night. She'd transformed herself into her Guardian form and gone to a club where older kids hung out.

To Irma's total surprise and delight, Andrew Hornby—an upperclassman who had never taken a second glance at dumpy little Irma—had suddenly become wildly attracted to her. It was all because Irma looked so different, so *absolutely gorgeous*, in her Guardian form.

Because she was so alluring, Irma had gotten to spend time with Andrew that night. She had talked to him as an equal, danced with him, flirted with him. Unfortunately, in the end, things had gone horribly wrong—so wrong, in fact, that Irma had ended up turning Andrew into a toad. It had been such a mess! The Guardians had had to scour the city to find him and turn him back into a boy again!

Andrew Hornby had noticed *Guardian* Irma, in a way he never would have noticed plain old regular Irma from middle school. That realization was starting to freak Cornelia out big-time! She couldn't help thinking, how will Caleb react when he sees the real me?

Cornelia realized that the only way she could know for sure was to transform right then and there in front of him. She could show herself to Caleb as she really was. But was she really ready for that? she questioned herself.

*Yes!* Cornelia boldly decided. She wanted Caleb to see her as she really was. It was the only way for him to truly understand her. And that was vitally important as they planned their future together.

But before Cornelia had a chance to act, Caleb was swept up in the debate among the members of the Congregation.

"Let us face the facts," said Tibor, addressing the Congregation in the Great Hall with a grim expression. "Things are looking bad for the citizens of Candracar, and no one has any idea how to stop Nerissa."

The chamber exploded with a dozen voices.

"We're doomed!" cried a citizen.

"This is the end of Candracar!" wailed another.

"There is no force strong enough to stand up

to the avenging Nerissa," exclaimed a third.

The Oracle raised his arms to silence them. "Calm down, please," he commanded, his level voice sailing over the babbling. "Let's wait to hear the Elders. Surely they have wisdom they can impart to us in this time of crisis."

Standing next to Cornelia, Caleb's eyes narrowed and he clenched his hand in a tight fist. "How many times have I seen situations like this?" he murmured with a frown. "If we don't act soon, it will be too late. Nerissa will be upon us, her minions circling this chamber on dark wings."

But Cornelia was not listening to Caleb's words, nor was she hearing the debate. A part of her knew that this was not the time or place to let her anxieties get the better of her. But she could not stop herself.

Sick with apprehension, obsessing over her future with Caleb, she decided she could no longer hide her true self from the man she loved. She simply could not wait to find out what Caleb thought of the real her!

With a wave of her hands, Cornelia transformed herself into the person she really was— a pretty but ordinary middle-school girl. What would Caleb think as he gazed at her, a simple human girl, smack in the middle of the Temple of Candracar? Maybe he would think that the Guardian spell had been canceled.

For a minute or two, Caleb did not notice what Cornelia had done. His attention was still riveted on the Congregation's debate over their plan of action in the coming struggle. "Even in Meridian," he told the Oracle, "it was difficult to keep our hopes up. But—"

Just then, he turned toward Cornelia. Suddenly, he saw her true form. Caleb's jaw slackened in shock. He squeezed his eyes shut and then opened them again. He shook his head, as if trying to clear the confusing vision from his mind. Finally, Caleb settled his astonished gaze on his beloved earth Guardian.

Cornelia stared. Her open, expectant gaze remained fixed on Caleb. His face was so handsome. His big, brown, long-lashed eyes were so fiery with his deeply felt need to protect the innocent and battle injustice.

Cornelia waited eagerly for those beautiful eyes to register their reaction. Of course, Cornelia expected immediate acceptance. She waited for Caleb to smile, to say something wonderful, to show her that he loved her in this form, too.

Within a minute, however, there was no doubt about Caleb's reaction to the real Cornelia. It was as big and bold and as easy to read as a *Heatherfield Daily* headline—and the news wasn't good.

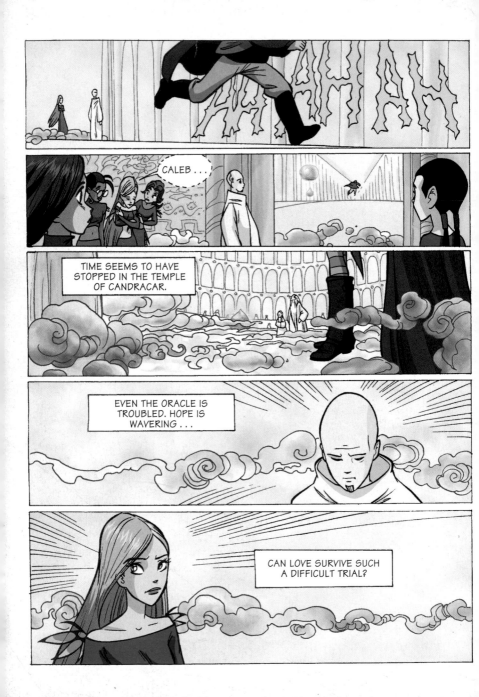

SOUNDS OF WAR ROCK THE REALM OF CANDRACAR. NO ONE KNOWS IF A NEW DAY WILL DAWN FOR THE TEMPLE.

TWO BRAVE HEARTS BEAT WITH DOUBT. WHAT WILL BECOME OF THEM?

AND HOW WILL THE GUARDIANS PERFORM WHEN THEY ARE CALLED UPON TO FACE THEIR MOST DIFFICULT CHALLENGE?

TO BE CONTINUED....